16 BANANAS

Also by Hugh Gross

SAME BED, DIFFERENT DREAMS

16 BANANAS

A Novel By
HUGH GROSS

M L P

Mid-List Press
Minneapolis

COPYRIGHT © 1995 by Hugh Gross

Published by Mid-List Press, 4324-12th Avenue South, Minneapolis, Minnesota 55407-3218

Library of Congress Cataloging-in-Publication Data
Gross, Hugh, 1955 -
16 bananas : a novel / by Hugh Gross
p.   cm.
ISBN 0-922811-21-0
I. Title   II. Title: Sixteen bananas.
PS3557.R575A615   1995
813' .54—dc20   94-23907   CIP

Banana design by Bill Rankin

Manufactured in the United States of America

Credits

I would like to thank my publisher, Marianne Nora. Her courage, sensitivity, humor, and goodwill made this book a reality. We also had a very good time along the way.

Jody Nolen, an editor at Mid-List Press, sent a notice to the *Yale Alumni Magazine* some years ago asking classmates to submit manuscripts. That note led to the publication of my first novel, *Same Bed, Different Dreams*. Jody's spirit and literary talents are deeply appreciated.

My brother David provided continuous encouragement as well as innumerable constructive suggestions with each consecutive draft. Many of my favorite lines are really his. He could not have been more helpful.

Aimee Liu, Cai Emmons, Arnold Margolin, and Eric Edson offered insight and lent support throughout the writing process. Others who made significant contributions to the book include Jolene Lee, Matt Bearson, Adam Blumenstein, Frank Gruber, Meredith Bilson, Robert Rotwein, Joan Goldfeder, Bill Bowling, Jonathan Taylor, John Levy, David Rosshirt, Jonathan Kaufelt, James Thornton, Richard Beale, Wendy Williams, Carl Bressler, Steven Clemons, Barbara Dalton-Taylor, and Robert Goldfarb.

And my parents, Mindy and Earl.

Dr. Norca,

This book is dedicated to you.

Thank you for making
this possible.

With All Best Wishes,

February 7, 1995

A Certain Angle

My first job in Hollywood was not in Hollywood but in Culver City, a municipality about ten miles southwest of downtown Los Angeles. I worked for a small company called Graphic Toner. From six in the morning until as close to noon as any of us could stand, we sold office supplies over the phone.

Telemarketing was not the work I had in mind when I moved from Cleveland to Los Angeles. I expected to enter immediately into my intended profession: directing feature films. But because I received no positive replies to the one-hundred twenty inquiry letters I sent to producers asking whether I might forward a videotape of the eight-minute film I had directed in my college filmmaking class, I was forced to face reality. And in this case reality meant that getting a job—any job—was preferable to returning home to family and friends in Cleveland having spent only one summer in pursuit of my dream.

Thinking back on that moment when I first arrived in Los Angeles, I realize just how naive I really was. I believed I had as good a chance to make it as anyone else did.

And when, with classified section in hand, I stepped into the basement of that faded yellow two-story building, the home of Graphic Toner, I kidded myself that I was simply in the wrong place at the right time.

"What is the difference between a triple bet and a trifecta?" my interviewer Howard Fingerman asked me.

"I have no idea," I said.

"You're hired. We'll teach you everything you need to know."

Howard then explained that an important part of my new job involved doing "little things" for him—such as running bets to the racetrack. Since I like to be up front with people from the get-go, I, in turn, explained to Howard that I had moved to Los Angeles because I wanted to be a film director. I told him that I didn't expect to be working at Graphic Toner for long, and if he didn't mind my taking an hour or two for irregular meetings or similarly excused absences in order to advance my career, I would be a very conscientious employee. Howard told me not to worry, adding that he was really a stand-up comedian himself.

Howard was unrivaled at Graphic Toner when it came to closing a sale. The most efficient way for him to work was to have someone else make his contact calls for him so that he would not have to waste time trying to get through to the right person. Howard said that there were plenty of leads, and when he showed me the Yellow Pages for Louisville, Kentucky, I could see he was right. If I ran out of leads in the Greater Louisville area, he pointed out, there were lots of other telephone books in Graphic Toner's library.

My job was to identify the person in charge of the copying machine in the office on the other end of the line. Then I would try to find out what kind of machine was being used. Generally I did this by assuming the persona of a fictional warehouse supervisor named Bob Daniels, asking with as much authority as possible for the copier's verification number. Since there is no such thing as a verification number on a copying machine, my question often created enough confusion for me to discover the machine's make and model number, which is what I really wanted to know in the first place.

At that point I would transfer the bewildered office manager to Ken White (aka Howard Fingerman), whom I identified as being the head of our accounting department. Howard would establish rapport through a few minutes of remarkably easy chitchat before changing gears and launching his sales pitch: our firm had accidently overshipped into the other company's territory, and we would therefore be able to offer a substantial discount on several boxes of toner for the very copier in question. Depending on how smoothly things went, Howard was sometimes able to sell copying paper, pens and pencils, coffee filters, and tea bags to the unsuspecting customer as well. More often than not, another two or three boxes from "the toner people" would be on their way out. Howard Fingerman was the greatest phone warrior Graphic Toner had ever known. He kept a sign above his desk that read: Eat shit and DI-al.

Howard operated strictly by headset. He used his hands to lend emphasis to his chatter, to type orders directly into the computer terminal on his desk, and to remind me through pantomime that I should be working. Using a headset also freed Howard to attack the *Daily Racing Form* with both hands. Judging by the many parimutuel tickets that papered the walls around his cubicle (and which represented only a fraction of the horses he had wagered on and lost), I'm not sure that two hands were any help. It turned out that Howard was the kind of horseplayer who often has one good idea about a race but insists on betting as if he has two.

Not all of our sales efforts were successful. There were times when, perhaps due to a prospect's previous run-in with another less than honorable telephone salesperson, Howard's advances met with little enthusiasm. He often ended those conversations by saying something crude, often about the other person's mother. For those office managers east of the Mississippi who may be wondering just who in California offered them those "win-win" discounts of fifty to sixty percent but shipped products marked up eight-hundred to twelve-hundred percent; or who, failing to make a sale, ended the conversation so rudely, there is a good chance that person was Howard Fingerman.

I mentioned that I like to be honest from the beginning. So I will admit that besides the wages (however minimal) and the performance bonuses (which I feared would be even more minimal), I enthusiastically accepted the position as Howard's assistant and stayed with that job for almost three years because of a woman named Madeline. She was, and for that matter probably still is, an aspiring actress who served nominally as Graphic Toner's office manager. To my untrained eye—what did I know?—Madeline seemed like the freest human being I had ever met.

Madeline's desk was positioned directly across from mine. On the two or three times a week she stopped by the office, often to pick up phone messages or something personal she had forgotten on a previous visit, she usually said hello to me. Madeline hardly ever noticed that I was staring at her face or her breasts because she did not pay a fraction of as much attention to me as I did to her. I do recall, however, that the few times she caught me looking, she did not seem to mind.

My status with Madeline improved over time. First, I was nonexistent. Then I became an unobtrusive fungus. Then I took up too much space. When I finally earned my wings in her estimation, I was trusted to "cover" for her. This was like being granted tenure at Graphic Toner. In marked contrast to the telephone calls I had been expected to make for Howard, I increasingly spent my mornings relaying phone messages, packaging toner for shipment, and dealing with irate customers. Although I cannot say I was ever really happy working at Graphic Toner, I was able to console myself from time to time with the fantasy that things could be worse.

There was one other person in that office who needs to be mentioned: Mike Curtis, the boss. His resumé included about two to three years of college and six to seven years in business. By the time I arrived on the scene, Mike was trying to avoid what looked like a sure two to five years each for tax evasion and fraud at Lompoc Federal Prison Camp.

In addition to owning Graphic Toner, Mike owned a photo studio, two check-cashing stores, thirty-nine pay telephones, and one very nice car. On those days when he showed up to work, we were often treated to a motivational pep talk. Mike's level of intensity, I soon learned, was closely related to his need for cash; his need for cash, in turn, was directly related to his need for cocaine. Once or twice during his more desperate hours, Mike got on the phone to sell toner himself. As I recall, he was not afraid to beg.

As luck would have it, Mike owned a piece of property just south of downtown. Of no particular value in itself—it was the site of a hamburger stand which had burned down suspiciously—the land did have some significance when viewed in a broader context. The property was adjacent to a much larger location, creating lucrative possibilities due to the access it afforded.

The larger piece of property was owned by parking lot magnate Sandy Fried, the brother of Phil Fried, the producer. Or perhaps I should say the former producer. As I would come to understand, though it was supposed to be a secret, Phil's livelihood was now much more closely linked to his brother Sandy's parking lot operations than to his own production of motion pictures. During the year-and-a-half it had taken to negotiate the purchase of Mike's hamburger-stand parcel, Phil served as the point man for the deal because Sandy would not deal directly with Mike.

Although it had been more than twelve years since Phil Fried produced a movie (and industry newcomers may be excused if they don't immediately recognize the name), he was still a well-liked and respected man—at least in some quarters. Phil was careful to maintain, if not burnish, an image as a can-do type of guy. In fact, when I was in a position to do some real asking, I learned that Phil Fried was a remarkably resourceful producer who had financed a number of small pictures beginning with little more than pocket change.

Perhaps Phil had arrived before his time. Had the more sophisticated markets for international theatrical, home video, cable, pay-per-view, and television existed when Phil sold his distribution rights, surely he would have been a lot better off financially. So Phil spent a considerable amount of energy making sure that people were aware of his uncredited contributions to movies like *The Godfather*, *Beverly Hills Cop*, *E.T.*, and *Jaws*. His actual credits appear on movies occasionally available for purchase in the bargain-bin section of neighborhood video stores.

On a number of occasions, I found myself running documents for Mike to Phil's office on Hollywood Boulevard because Mike didn't want to speak to Phil, who himself had been enlisted in the deal because Sandy didn't want to speak to Mike.

The first time I met Phil, he was shuffling papers next to a file cabinet in his private office. He greeted me with a big smile. "How's your dad?" he asked.

"Fine." I wondered why he cared. "I haven't spoken with him in a few days."

"Your father represented me during my first divorce, did he tell you?"

"No."

"Your father is one hell of an attorney, let me tell you. My ex-wife wanted the condo in Palm Springs. We had a second mortgage on it at fifteen percent, callable in three years—"

"But," I said, "my father's an orthodontist."

"Aren't you Stern?" Phil asked. "Harold Stern?"

"No."

"Who are you?"

I remember having a split-second debate in my mind about whether to introduce myself as an aspiring director. "My name is Sheldon Green. I have an envelope for you from Mike Curtis." By saying "for you" I was trying to warm things up without overdoing it.

"Who?"

"Sheldon Green."

"No. Mike who?"

"Mike Curtis. I think this is about a piece of property downtown."

"You can put it over there." He waved his hand in the general direction of an unoccupied desk out front.

"By the way," I asked, "where's the best place to park around here?"

"Wherever you can. Thanks."

A slender, attractive woman, perhaps thirty, entered the room as I left. On my way to the elevator I could hear Phil lecturing her about the need to establish a system so that not just anybody could walk into his private office.

On my next visit a young man wearing thick, round glasses sat at the formerly unoccupied desk. There were three or four screenplays spread in front of him. He looked at me. "May I ask what this is in reference to?"

"I have a package for Philip S. Fried," I said. "May I speak with him?"

"Mr. Fried is out right now. Kimberley will be back in a few minutes."

"Who's Kimberley?" I asked.

"Kimberley is Mr. Fried's secretary. Why don't you leave it with me? My name is Harold Stern. I do everything around here."

"Oh? How long have you worked for Mr. Fried?"

"About a week." Harold stuck out his hand, and we shook.

"This is an important delivery," I said, unsure how else to advance my career other than to personally hand this envelope to Philip S. Fried, who once made movies.

"Mr. Fried is in Beverly Hills."

Whatever system Phil and Kimberley believed that they had set up to enforce privacy, Harold Stern was not a strong choice to enforce it. Harold compensated for not knowing the answer to a simple question, such as why

Phil was in Beverly Hills, by eagerly dispensing all kinds of information he obviously should never have been entrusted with or at least should have known not to pass along.

When Phil returned to his office forty-five minutes later, I already knew more than I needed to know about him. For example, in my first conversation with Harold, I learned that Phil was financially on the ropes, barely hanging on, and pitifully unable to compete in a business he claimed was "deserting" him.

About a week later, in our second conversation, Harold told me that Phil's third divorce settlement had been the killer, an agreement which left Phil with crushing support payments, in addition to all the obligations he still carried from his second divorce. Harold was quick to point out that neither the second nor third agreements had been negotiated by his father who, needless to say, had been relatively effective in handling the first, or Harold and I would not have been speaking. Harold was honest enough to tell me that the main reason he had been hired was Phil's regret at not having retained Harold's father—or an attorney as effective as Harold's father—to handle Divorce Numbers Two and Three.

"Maybe he thinks about it unconsciously," I suggested, hoping to give Harold an out in terms of his self-esteem.

"Maybe he thinks about it consciously," Harold replied.

According to Harold, Phil's lapse in judgment regarding Divorce Attorneys Two and Three ran through his mind like a continuously looped tape. Phil held the two lawyers responsible not only for his strapped cash position, but also for the crummy office he occupied in a run-down part of Hollywood, which had a lease he could not afford to give up. During a period when the industry had moved to Beverly Hills, Century City, and Studio City, Phil had been left behind in the worst part of Hollywood, an area as blighted as New York's Times Square.

Harold suggested that it wasn't the lack of an over-sized expense account or the need for a prestigious address that was really hurting Phil these days, but rather his inability to invest sufficiently in "development."

"'Development?'" I asked. "What's that?"

Harold defined the term in the following manner: "A producer options or acquires the rights to a property for as little money as possible; convinces a writer to adapt, write, and rewrite the material—again, for as little money as possible; entertains and entices potential financiers and distributors—always, but with difficulty, for as little money as possible; and then sells out to someone else for as much money as possible, as soon as possible."

For the first time, I felt like I understood what the movie business was really all about. In fact, I felt as if I understood the whole world more clearly.

According to Harold, the most painful consequence of Phil's mismanagement was his nearly complete financial dependence on his brother Sandy. Without a doubt, Harold insisted, Phil had been far more successful over the last five or six years raising funds from people in the entertainment world for investment in Sandy's parking lots than in any entertainment-related activities of his own.

Harold speculated that Phil's financial problems were further complicated because most of what he did still own in the world was tied up as equity in his brother's parking lots. And one of the keys to Sandy's success was that he held on to the properties he owned like a child protects his toys. For Sandy Fried, the parking lot business was a real-

life game of Monopoly in which he bought every property he landed on and never sold.

Harold told me so many personal things about Phil
Fried in our first two conversations that I wondered if Phil
hadn't done something to make Harold resent him. Let's
face it, a person doesn't usually go into this kind of detail
regarding someone he or she truly respects. But on further
consideration, I suppose it was simply a matter of person-
alities and not anything that Phil had done to Harold.

This much was clear: I wasn't the only one who had a
few things to learn.

Busy, No Income

The next time I arrived with a delivery for Phil, Harold's desk was unoccupied.

"Where's Harold?" I asked Kimberley.

"Harold no longer works here."

"What happened?"

"I'm not allowed to discuss it."

"I won't tell anyone."

"I said I'm not allowed to discuss it. Why are you even asking me?"

"I consider Harold Stern to be a friend. I'm just wondering what happened."

"Well, if Harold Stern is a friend of yours, then he can tell you what happened himself."

"Fair enough," I said. "In the meantime, you don't know if Phil is looking for someone to replace Harold, do you?"

"I don't know. I'll ask him, if you like, when he's here and I have a chance."

"Thanks."

I gave Kimberley both my work and home phone numbers so she could call me as soon as she had the word.

I must have been back and forth to Phil's office three or four more times with documents related to the property sale. Each time Phil was out. Finally, with the transaction about to close, I walked in one day and noticed Phil sitting behind his desk staring vacantly into space.

"Hi, Kimberley," I said. "How are you?"

"Good."

"I don't mean to push, but I was wondering if you'd had a chance to ask Phil whether he plans to hire anybody to fill Harold's old job."

"Oh," she responded quickly. "Just a second." She disappeared into Phil's office, closing the door behind her.

When Kimberley returned, she explained that the position entailed a considerable amount of telephone prospecting to members of the entertainment community regarding financial investment. She said that the job was hardly as glamorous as it seemed and that they had made a mistake in not explaining this thoroughly enough to Harold, who seemed only to be interested in reading and reviewing the many screenplays that managed to find their way into the office. Kimberley emphasized that the ability to keep one's mouth shut was of paramount importance to Phil and that he didn't want to hire someone who was going to come in and write a book about the whole thing. She confided that when Harold left, they had offered to try to find him another position somewhere else, but it had all been too much for the guy. She said that Harold left fighting tears, vowing to enroll in law school at the first opportunity. Kimberley giggled. "What do you think?" she asked me. "Does the job sound reasonable?"

"Yes!" I said. I was relieved that I hadn't shown impatience or become angry with Kimberley upon learning she had forgotten about my earlier request completely. Every day, during the last six weeks, I had been anxiously awaiting her call. Does the job sound reasonable? I asked myself. What difference does it make?

Phil appeared at the door to his office. "Hold my calls," he instructed Kimberley. He looked at me briefly, then turned to go back inside.

I stood by Kimberley's desk, waiting for instructions.

"Yes," she said wearily.

I pointed at Phil's office.

"Yes," she said. "Go in."

Phil began by discussing the virtues of parking lot investment. A person can see where the money goes. It's not a high-tech product that's difficult to understand.

I tried to score points by intimating that I had once counseled Mike Curtis on the wisdom of releasing the hamburger-stand property when Mike had been wavering. I managed to work the word "commitment" into my speech.

Phil took a long look at me. I felt as if he could see right through me. God, I was such a fake. It's true that I had congratulated Mike when the property was officially in escrow. It didn't seem unnatural to play up my small role in the transaction. Certainly there should be some reward for being associated with the deal. Retreating before Phil's glare, I heard myself trying to reassure him that my experience at Graphic Toner was good preparation for the work I would be doing in his office.

Phil cautioned me that my experience at Graphic Toner was only marginally related to what I would do for him and more likely to be of no use at all. It might even work to my disadvantage, he warned, since I'd undoubtedly picked up any number of bad habits in the other office. But Phil said that it wasn't fair to hold this against me. "Why don't we take it from the top?" he asked.

Phil insisted that style meant a lot to the people he did business with and that a low-key style was best. "When you're on the phone, this is what you say: 'As busy as Phil Fried is, he has asked me to inform you that another terrific investment opportunity has come up.'" He added that I could use a specific number—twenty—one time in regard to after-tax percentage return on investment, but after that, I should fall back on such general expressions as "above average," "not to mention the tax benefits," and "of course, past performance does not guarantee future results."

I noticed that during this run-through, in contrast to the treatment I had been receiving only a few moments before, Phil was not even looking at me when he spoke. Although I found this confusing, it did occur to me that if he wasn't going to pay attention to me, then maybe I didn't have to pay so much attention to him. It's true that I was in no position to assume such a reckless attitude, but since Phil managed to repeat each point at least three times, how much could he have been expecting?

I thought about Howard Fingerman. God knows if anyone was truly qualified for the job, it was Howard. Not only that, he had been complaining about the dead-end nature of life at Graphic Toner. His sales were down, too, but not because he had lost any of his technical prowess, I was sure. Rather Howard had finally succumbed to the Graphic Toner malaise, an abandonment of any pretense of belief in the value of hard work and a surrender to the notion that life is better enjoyed when doing nothing at all. I mention this because in a more honorable or just world, I would surely have disqualified myself from consideration and recommended my friend and mentor Howard Fingerman as Harold Stern's successor. If nothing else, however, I recognized that the world is neither honorable nor just. Phil Fried was offering me a job. I was thrilled to accept it.

Phil welcomed me aboard with a more specific discussion related to two points, the first of which concerned my pay. Ominously, he began by saying that he had offered the job to Kimberley when Harold left, but she didn't want to take a pay cut. He continued by proposing flexibility with my schedule as compensation for the meager wages I would receive. As we were getting down to numbers, Phil actually encouraged me to keep my job at Graphic Toner, suggesting that by juggling two jobs I could better maintain my income until things took off for me in his office. The truth is that I didn't care about the money. I could now claim—if not to myself, then to family and friends back home—that I was working in the entertainment business. My feelings about returning to Cleveland after three years in California were remarkably similar to the feelings I had at the end of my first summer in Los Angeles when I realized I had to get a job or go home. I wasn't going back.

Phil's second point raised the question of loyalty, something he said that he demanded absolutely and that he was willing to reciprocate in kind. "Did Harold Stern ever speak to you about the goings-on in this office?" he asked me.

"No."

"Then we'll leave it at that. The things you see and hear while you work here are nobody's business but our own. Is that clear?"

I nodded.

"Are you sure you understand?"

"Yes."

"Absolutely?"

"I'm loyal," I said, hoping I would not betray the extent to which I had already learned that loyalty in Los Angeles and the film business was a concept that came with all kinds of qualifications. "I'll do whatever you ask me to do."

Phil told me that I could begin as soon as I liked, but stressed once more the purpose of my new position. He said there could be no question about why I was there. "Everybody in this town wants to be a producer or director. Nobody wants to hear about your interests. You have to take a number. There are a lot of people who have been around here longer than you have. The best thing is to keep your eyes open and your mouth shut. I'm not being mean. It's the same advice I got when I started, and it's served me well."

Given Phil's position in life, which could hardly be described as an unqualified success, I took his advice with the proverbial grain of salt. That is, I made a mental note and tried not to laugh.

I confess that I may have just drawn a harsh portrait of Phil Fried. And maybe something about the man calls out for such criticism. But there is one thing I should mention: a picture of Phil in serviceman's uniform that stood on a bookshelf in the farthest corner of his office. Although I did ask on several occasions, Phil was reluctant to talk about his war experiences. In truth, I would have guessed that Phil Fried was the type of person who dodged his military responsibility or served in less than a frontline capacity. But this was not the case at all. Phil served as an infantryman in Europe in World War II during some of the heaviest fighting of the war.

The following Monday, my first day on the job, I arrived at eight. Kimberley showed up about nine-fifteen.

"Have you been waiting long?" she asked.

"Ten minutes," I said.

"We'll have to make you some keys."

As Kimberley turned on the lights, I told her that the office manager where I used to work was also an actress. But the introduction I proposed so that Madeline and Kimberley could compare notes over drinks seemed to be of little interest.

Phil arrived at ten. He announced that he wanted to see me right away in his office. I assumed that memories of the Harold Stern fiasco were fresh in his mind and I would be given clear marching orders. Instead, I sat in front of Phil's desk while he opened his mail and answered an incessant stream of phone calls. Phil discussed the weekend box office results; debated the pro's and con's (mostly con's) of a science fiction remake of *Casablanca*; ascertained the availability of certain major stars; speculated on the direction of real estate, precious metals, and the stock market; and endorsed the value of massaging a little jojoba oil into the scalp before going to bed.

Phil explained the difference between perception and reality. "Two sides of the same con."

Although Phil seemed content to yak away on the phone while I sat and watched, he did occasionally cast an eye my way. At one point, he thrust a copy of *Daily Variety* in my direction.

I made a game of guessing how Phil's phone conversations would end, but there wasn't much to it. Phil invariably concluded by saying either, "You'll get back to me on that, right?" or "Let me know what happens."

"Do you read it?" Phil asked me during a break between calls.

"*Variety*?"

"*Variety*," Phil confirmed.

"Sometimes," I said. Meaning I hadn't, but I would from now on.

"You should read it every day. Never here, but at home."

"I will," I said.

"You can learn an incredible amount by reading the trades. Choose one—*Variety* or *The Hollywood Reporter*—and make it your Bible."

"All right," I said. "I'll do that."

"Or both. Read them both every day. That's better."

I nodded.

Phil reached back and handed me a thicker *Variety*, which he took from a pile on top of the credenza behind his desk. "*Weekly Variety*. It comes out once a week. You should read that, too."

"Thanks," I said. "I will."

"The Bible," he repeated. He looked at his watch. "Have you eaten?"

"No."

"It's early, but what the hell. I'm hungry. Kimberley!"

She appeared in the doorway. "What is it?"

"Chinese. What do you think? Is it too early? I'm starving."

"It's not too early. It's eleven-thirty. Which place?"

"What do you think, down the street or around the corner?"

"Down the street is faster. Around the corner is better."

"Let's have around the corner then. We want to impress the newest member of our team, no?"

"Anything in particular?"

Phil looked at me.

"I'm easy."

"The usual then. No MSG. Order something special in honor of our guest. Make it a surprise. We have Cokes in the fridge?"

She nodded.

"All right. Make sure they put it all in the wonton soup. *Wor* wonton soup, right? I want everything."

"I understand," Kimberley said. "You know it was *wor* wonton soup last time. They just didn't put enough of the other stuff in."

"Case closed," Phil said. "You have cash?"

"I think there's some left. I'll check, but it should be enough." Kimberley left.

Phil turned to me. "Did you notice the way that Kimberley felt compelled to make an excuse about the wonton soup? I've mentioned it to her. She's not going to succeed in this business if she doesn't break that habit. Excuses don't mean anything. Let me give you an example. How much money did you make last year?"

"I—"

Phil interrupted. "I don't care how much money you made last year. That's not the point. What's important is how you answered the question. You may not be aware, but when I asked, you hesitated. Don't ever make excuses. Just answer. If all you're doing is holding things together, tell people that life is exciting and it's all you can do to hold it together. After that, tell them you've got a few irons in the fire. You know, it's almost gotten to the point that every other question people ask in this town boils down to how much money you're making.

"One of the beautiful things about the motion picture business," Phil continued, "is that you're only so far away from a start date at any given time. It doesn't matter how long it's been. A decent premise, some financing, a little bit of luck . . . you're on top. I know they say everything takes ten million years, but it's not necessarily so. Name a great movie."

"*The Wizard of Oz.*"

"That is a great movie, but it's too easy. I want something more contemporary."

"*Raiders of the Lost Ark.*"

Phil nodded. He closed his eyes. "A sympathetic archaeologist confounds Nazis and reconciles with an old flame while in search of an ancient relic with implications for the future of mankind." He opened his eyes. "How complicated was that? The audience goes to the theater and they see an actor chased by a huge bowling ball. The picture makes millions of dollars. You don't have to be a genius to succeed in this business. You don't *want* to be a genius to succeed in this business!

"I got a call the other day from a producer who told me he was making a different kind of movie. And I said, before he could even tell me what the picture was about, 'Different? Who wants different?' This business is not about different. It's about coming in under budget with a product people want to see. And believe me, what people want to see is not something different. It's something mostly the same. Only a little bit different. Do you follow me?"

"I think so."

"You want to direct. All right. Have you thought about the kind of movie you'd like to make one day?"

"I want to make films that have a social impact."

"Social impact?" Phil paused. "Social impact? All right. There's nothing wrong with social impact. But be more specific. What exactly do you mean when you say 'social impact?'"

"I'd like to make a movie about Martin Luther King,"
I said, "although I realize that would be difficult to do
well."

"Difficult, shmifficult," Phil said, lowering his head
and looking around the room to make sure he would not
be overheard. "Difficult is not the problem. Difficulty is
something we can deal with. The problem is audience.
That stuff is death at the box office. Nobody wants to see
it. If your definition of 'social impact' is a movie nobody
wants to see, go to film school. As a matter of fact, I'm not
sure they'll let you make a picture like that in film school
these days either. What people want to see is a picture that
makes them feel good, that's what they want. Every day
people fight their way through traffic to get to jobs that
they hate. When they get home, they don't want to think
about what's troubling them or what's wrong with the
world. They want to forget those things. They want to
have a good time. And if they can't actually enjoy themselves for ninety minutes, at least they want to forget
about their problems. Be distracted. And they're willing to
pay for the privilege. What's so terrible about that?"

The way Phil was looking at me, I imagined he wanted a response. "Nothing," I said. "I guess."

"You don't have to guess," he said. "I know. Now close
your eyes."

I did.

"It's your birthday. You're five years old. All your
friends are seated at the table. Suddenly, there's a hush.
You turn around and your mother is carrying a birthday
cake with candles. It's for you!"

I nodded.

"See if you can hold that feeling."

"I'll try," I said.

"That's what we're looking for. That's what we want. All right, you can open your eyes now."

Phil activated his telephone and hit an automatic dial code. "Conference call," he said. "Do you know who Max Planck is?"

I thought for an instant. "Wasn't he a famous physicist?"

"I'm talking about Max Planck, the producer. Major player."

"Max Planck's office," a woman said on the other end of the line.

"Is he there?" Phil asked.

"Who is it, please?"

"Is he there?"

"Who is it?"

Phil winked at me. "It's Phil Fried."

"What company, please, Mr. Fried?"

"Phil Fried," Phil repeated. "He knows who I am."

"Oh, Mr. Fried," the secretary said. "I'm sorry. The parking lots—of course. Mr. Planck is in a meeting right now. Would you like to leave a message?"

"Ask Max to call me," Phil said. "Nothing urgent."

"Of course, Mr. Fried. I'll let him know that you called."

"Max Planck is in on the parking lots," Phil told me when the dial tone sounded again on his speaker phone. "Sometimes his secretary gets confused."

Kimberley entered carrying two bags of Chinese food.

"Here," Phil said, tapping a finger on his desk. "Do I love Chinese food. Put it all down right here."

"*Wor* wonton soup, *mu shu* chicken, house special fried rice," Kimberley said. She juggled a large cylindrical container filled with soup, several other white paper containers full of food, and three cans of Coke. Setting them down, the container of soup spilled. Shrimp, water chest-nuts, Chinese pea pods, ham, chicken, wontons, and a murky light-colored broth poured onto Phil's desk.

"Shit!" Kimberley said.

She tried to clean up the mess using the napkins which came with the food. When that wasn't enough, she pulled a handkerchief from her purse. It was a losing battle. "I'll be right back," she said.

Phil turned my way. "Give her a hand," he barked. "Here. Use the *Variety*!"

Not So Busy, No Income

I thought Phil and I were off to a good start. He spoke incessantly about movie deals, wives, ex-wives, therapists, ex-therapists, secrets of the universe, and so on. That's why it struck me as odd when, within a month, I was forced to suffer not only the silent treatment, but I could hardly engage his attention at all. Even the list of names I was supposed to receive so I could begin making my prospecting calls was not forthcoming.

The few times Phil did ask me a question, I could tell he wasn't interested in hearing what I had to say. It was just a ruse so that he could answer himself.

Nobody at Graphic Toner was speaking to me either— at least not with any kindness. When I stopped by to see if my final check was ready, Howard referred to me loudly as "that little asshole who thinks he's hit the big time." Mike Curtis asked me what I was doing on the premises. I did make a point to ask both Mike and Howard how things were going. I offered to find my own replacement. These gestures didn't help. At least Madeline was consistent. She didn't care.

The "big time" at Phil Fried's meant sitting at an empty desk, fully aware that Phil could see me through his open office door. I tried to occupy my time by creating errands and chores. I was afraid to do anything that wasn't job-related, but I didn't have much to do that was. My first substantive accomplishment was to track down Harold Stern and arrange to give him his last paycheck. I worked on this for about a week before leaving the envelope with a receptionist at his father's office in the Mid-Wilshire district.

I would hardly say it was an easy time. I was usually first to arrive in the morning. I always stayed until Phil and Kimberley left. I wasn't doing anything, but I thought it was important to create the right impression. I figured that on the rare occasion when Phil would call from outside to ask about something he'd forgotten, or for his phone messages, my presence would be noted. One time, Phil did ask me to run an important folder he'd left lying on his desk to a meeting in West Los Angeles. I wasn't invited to sit in, but I could tell Phil appreciated having someone around who could deliver the goods.

When Phil was out of the office, I could relax. If Kimberley was up for a part, I didn't mind, I enjoyed reading lines with her. I'd learned at Graphic Toner about the value of "covering" for someone else. I believe Kimberley took me into her confidence as soon as she understood I could be trusted this way.

Kimberley taught me a few lessons regarding office politics. The main thing I learned from her was that it's never a mistake to treat work as another form of performance art. She explained the three-act structure. Morning is Act I. Afternoon is Act II. Act III begins sometime between five and six-thirty.

After several months, it struck me that Phil didn't care whether I was working or not. I don't want to oversimplify this point. Phil is definitely results-oriented. But regardless of what he said when I signed on about concentrating my efforts on the parking lots, Phil needed to see me as part of a larger framework, a vision that involved his making motion pictures again. It might be true that Sandy's parking lots had become his bread-and-butter through the last lean years, but even Phil needed to dream. And if my making sales calls to raise money for limited partnerships was going to disturb his reverie then so be it, I wouldn't make them. Larger forces were at work on my behalf, I speculated. I just hoped those forces knew what they were doing. God knows Phil didn't.

Understanding my position in Phil's cosmos took some pressure off me, although my days were still maddeningly slow. I enjoyed hearing the snippets of conversation which occasionally floated out of his private office. "Why don't you two get into bed on this and see how it feels to wiggle your toes?" Phil asked someone on the phone.

One afternoon I misunderstood Kimberley and thought that Steven Spielberg himself was on hold. Instead, it was a bookkeeper in his business manager's office calling about K-whatever tax forms they were supposed to have received from Sandy, sent to the wrong address for the second year in a row. I felt I handled this call very professionally, redirecting the bookkeeper to Sandy's office.

But the main skill I was developing was the ability to do nothing smoothly. In fact, I was getting to be pretty good at it.

Around this time, I began to drop by a photography store down the street from Phil's office. I've always had an interest in photography, it's somewhat related to the craft of making motion pictures, I had a lot of time to kill, and an extremely cute girl worked there. I won't say that she encouraged me, but she didn't discourage me either. At one point, I suspected she liked me because she seemed to avoid my glance whenever I looked her way; I thought she might be ignoring me on purpose. On the job a person is supposed to concentrate on work. It wouldn't have been appropriate for her to socialize with me during business hours. Also, it was a busy store and it seemed that there were always a couple of customers around in addition to the two older male employees who acted as if they had a big brother relationship with her. They were always hovering nearby when I tried to isolate her in a way that I could make conversation about F-stops and ASA numbers and custom labs, and why don't the two of us take our cameras and go on a hike together this weekend?

I finally got an opportunity to speak to this woman one afternoon while walking back to my office after lunch. I noticed that she was in the store by herself so I entered. She seemed eager to talk and she knew all about F-stops and ASA numbers and custom labs.

"What's your name?" I asked.

"Rhonda."

"My name is Sheldon. How long have you lived in Los Angeles?"

Rhonda then proceeded to tell me about her roommate, her boyfriend, how she missed her family in Arizona, and how hard it was to live in Los Angeles without a car. She told me she had driven here, but that her car's engine had since blown. She claimed she was both too broke and too lazy to find another one. I expressed surprise at how well she had been able to manage without transportation.

Rhonda and I quickly established the kind of mutual likes (baseball, the environment, going to movies), and dislikes (corporations that destroy the environment, people who complain about life but watch TV all day, politicians who will say anything to get elected) that ordinarily lead to a lunch, if not a more serious date. Then she asked me what I did for a living.

I told her that I was an aspiring director. I said I had a few irons in the fire and that I was trying to hold everything together working temporarily for a well-known producer while waiting for something good to happen. Seeing her reaction made me consider the possibility that she was going to scream and run out of the store. She didn't actually say anything. She didn't have to. Judging by the severity of her facial expression, I could tell that she must have had some kind of negative experience before. I decided I could also use some work on my delivery.

One of the older male employees entered the store carrying a bag of take-out food and a soft drink. Rhonda asked me if I had any other questions about cameras. I felt so anxious, I was relieved to go.

When I returned to the office, Kimberley directed me to join Phil who was speaking with a man I thought looked a lot like Elvis Presley. I'm not sure why I was invited in. Kimberley didn't say. I didn't ask.

"I'd like to have that phone number," Phil said to his guest as I entered. "Only a certain type of foreign investor antes up for a screenplay as ridiculous as that one."

Phil positioned his right hand in the shape of a gun. "Bobby Savino," he said to the purple polyester puffery seated on the other side of his desk, "meet Sheldon Green."

We shook hands.

"Bobby invented a tennis ball you can use in the rain," Phil said.

"Really?" I asked.

"The only problem," Phil continued, "was that nobody did."

I didn't think this was so funny, but Bobby and Phil had a pretty good yuk.

"Bobby was a record producer," Phil said. "A very successful promoter who got lucky with a couple music-related films." He winked at Bobby. "Now he wants into the real movie business. He's sitting on a screenplay he likes."

"Something you wrote?" I asked.

"Of course not," Phil said as if I had just passed gas in his office. "He has the rights to a script."

"What's it about?"

"Shakespeare wrote the first draft," Phil said. He and Bobby laughed again.

"Have you heard of Prince?" Bobby asked me.

"Sure," I said, "the musician."

Bobby nodded. "We're going to get Prince to do the music. My brother-in-law is friends with a girl Prince has been dating."

"Why don't you get Brooke Shields, too?" Phil asked. "I hear Prince is finished these days." Phil raised his eyebrows and looked at me for confirmation.

I was about to say that I would take Brooke Shields any day of the week, when Bobby spoke.

"Then we'll get someone else," he said. "Less aggravation. I won't have to worry if he finds a new girlfriend."

"That's all you need," Phil said, "to be worrying about Prince's love life. Your blood pressure is going to be high enough as it is."

"That's true," Bobby nodded. "My blood pressure is very high already."

"How's Alice?" Phil asked.

"You didn't know?" Bobby seemed genuinely surprised.

"Don't tell me . . . What?"

"We separated."

"How am I supposed to know?" Phil exclaimed. "Christ!" He moved to another chair and put one hand on his forehead. "You crazy son-of-a-bitch. You move to California where they kill you when you get a divorce. You should have taken care of it in New Jersey before you moved to California."

"It's not so easy getting a divorce in Jersey these days, either."

Phil sighed. "What happened? I always thought if ever there was a lock it was you and Alice."

"I thought so myself," Bobby replied. "Apparently I said the wrong thing."

I noticed that Phil was not wearing his wedding ring, which may have been a timely observation considering he spent the next fifteen minutes delivering an insider's view of divorce.

"In my first divorce," Phil explained, "I had very good counsel. I bought my wife out.

"In my next divorce," he continued, "I was forced to commit to regular payments and I also gave up 'net points.' You know what that means: she keeps a percentage of my future income, after expenses.

"My ex-wife was pleased. On paper it looked as if she was getting a good deal. Of course there haven't been any big profits, but even if there were, there are so many ways to manipulate my expenses, she would never see her share of the bonus pool anyway."

Phil was quick to add that this had still been a painful transaction. "I failed to anticipate how debilitating monthly payments can be," he explained. "Like a second mortgage, but without the new kitchen."

His third wife got the equivalent of "an adjusted gross deal." "I take a little off the top for groceries. She takes a healthy slice of the rest. I swore I would never get divorced again, but then I fell in love. What a mistake that was!"

Phil declared that now he was hitched for life. "I can't afford another divorce," he moaned. "There's nothing left." His fourth and current wife made him sign a prenuptial agreement guaranteeing her a piece of the action whether she's around or not.

"Prenuptial with back-end participation?!" Bobby gasped. "Nobody gets that anymore!"

"Pay or play," Phil confirmed. "Like a schmuck I went for it."

Bobby said that when you hear about someone else going through a separation or divorce you never think twice. "But when it's happening to you, it's not so easy. My wife and I were going to a marriage counselor. I thought things were getting better. Then boom. She moves out and she's gone."

"There's only one problem with therapy," Phil said. "It doesn't work. Four times a week for more than three years I went to an analyst who worked out of a house overlooking the ocean. If I had gone to the bank and filled a wheelbarrow full of hundred dollar bills, I could have dumped it in the water—at least I would have saved the time." He paused. "This therapist was good with certain kinds of dreams, though. And she did know a lot about masturbation."

Bobby said that the hardest part was not knowing whether to be nice to his wife when she stopped by to pick up her things. And whether to forward her mail and pay her bills, especially her therapist's bill, or to be mean and try to make her life more difficult. "You'd think that acting like an asshole would be the natural thing to do given the circumstances," he said, "but when she's around I don't feel that way."

"You want to get back together with her again," Phil said.

"I don't know anymore. Maybe."

"You do," Phil said, "but trust me. Things will never be the same. She's probably sleeping with her therapist."

"She's not sleeping with her therapist."

"It was a bad joke," Phil said.

"Say whatever you want," Bobby replied.

"All right." Phil gave Bobby some pointers relating to the specifics of his upcoming settlement. Among other things he told Bobby to ask for a percentage of his wife's future income if she was going to get the same. "My second wife owns three nightclubs and a cooking school now. All I had to do was ask, I could have had a piece of the action."

Bobby appeared ready to change the subject. "What do you do, kid?" he asked me.

"He's a director," Phil answered. "In the meantime, he's helping me with the parking lots."

"Ever directed anything?"

"What does that matter?" Phil asked. "You've seen the kind of movies they're making these days."

"If I were starting out again and wanted to direct . . . I don't know. You have to write something that somebody wants to produce. Otherwise, it's catch-22. Who's going to hire a director who hasn't directed before? Phil, you know this. Am I right? Has he written anything?"

"He wants to make movies that will have a positive social impact," Phil said. "He's working on a screenplay about Martin Luther King."

"I haven't really started," I said.

"*Ghandi* was a big hit," Bobby said.

Phil snorted and rolled his eyes.

"Phil, what is it? Why are you laughing?" Bobby asked. "First screenplays have to be written. You know that. I wouldn't be discouraged, kid. It's hard. It's true there's more money out there these days, but there's also more competition. You have to knock on every door. You can't take no for an answer. You have to make people realize that you're special. Persistence. Some things in life will never change."

"I have a videotape of a film I directed in college. It's only eight minutes long. Can I send it to you?"

"Sure," Bobby said. "But let me save you the trouble. I'm not in the market. It's nothing personal. Some people would give you a line here, string you along. Now if I get this current project set up, I'm going to be in position to do a lot of things. I'll be looking for material then."

"He'll be looking for material," Phil repeated. "You can send it to him then."

Bobby nodded.

"By the way," Phil asked Bobby, "who's handling your paperwork?"

"We haven't gotten to that point. I mean Alice and I are still not absolutely sure."

"You better get somebody fast," Phil said. "I can recommend some people you shouldn't use. But that's not what I meant. Who's handling the paperwork on your screenplay option?"

"Aaron Wexler."

"Aaron Wexler?" Phil grimaced. "At Hannibal and Cox?"

Bobby nodded. "Why?"

Phil rubbed his chin.

"What is it?"

"I'm not sure I should say."

"Say."

"You're talking about an attorney," Phil said, "who looks for the nice people in the world, the ones who like to cooperate, and thinks up ways to screw them."

"Sounds good," Bobby said. "You want a social worker representing you?"

"I want someone who isn't going to turn around and stab me in the back."

"Did he do that to you?"

"Maybe he did," Phil said, "and maybe he didn't. I'll tell you this much. That man is slime."

"So what? Do you have any idea who he represents? He's made a ton of money for his clients."

"He's made a ton of money for *some* of his clients," Phil corrected Bobby. "Do you know what it means to have an attorney-client relationship?"

"Of course."

"Well, your relationship with this guy will last as long as you're paying him. After that, everything he knows about you and what you're doing he'll use for himself and his other clients. If your option runs out, he'll probably shop the property all over town."

"Is that legal?" Bobby asked.

"I didn't say he wasn't smart. I said the man is slime."

"Funny," Bobby said, "he seemed like such a nice guy. I'd heard nothing but good things."

"He is a nice guy," Phil said. "So am I."

"Your wife is on the line," Kimberley interrupted from the doorway. "I didn't know whether to take a message."

Phil picked up the phone. Mostly he listened. "Honey," he said finally, "seven-thirty or eight . . . what difference does it make what time the maid comes? Make a decision and stick with it." He hung up. "Christ, no wonder it takes her twenty-five minutes to use the bathroom. What were we talking about?"

"The business," Bobby answered.

"It's a good business," Phil said. "We make money because some people think what we do is unimportant. But it's prestigious because other people think it *is* important."

"I don't know," Bobby said. "I don't know if it's such a good business anymore. Things have changed. What do you think, kid?"

"He's too young to think," Phil said. "Give him a little time."

"Yeah," Bobby said, "we could all use a little time."

If Bobby arrived that day with something specific in mind, he sure didn't sell it directly. On the other hand, I'm not sure he would have had a chance. Phil might not have enjoyed much of the limelight himself in recent years, but he was certainly an expert when it came to undercutting other people. If he didn't like an idea or was bored, he was quick to lay down a line, the psychological impact of which was the kiss of death. For example, when someone else was enthusiastic about a project, Phil liked to say, "It's good. I just don't know if it's commercial."

Of course, if Phil was pitching something and was challenged this way, he was quick to respond, often with the look of a wounded fox, "It's a fantasy. Use your imagination!" And if the other person remained unconvinced, Phil might go on the attack. "I said it was a fantasy. That's what movies are all about. How long are you planning to work in this business?"

When Bobby left, Phil and Kimberley had a fight about how we were buying copier paper. Kimberley suggested that if we bought larger amounts less often we could save money. Phil grumbled about the paper we were wasting.

Since this was an area I knew something about, I tried to mediate. They weren't interested in anything I had to say.

"Do whatever you want," Phil told Kimberley finally. "I have too much on my mind to worry about blank sheets of paper. I'm going back to the gridlock on my desk. Hold my calls."

The phone rang.

"Mr. Fried is in a meeting," Kimberley said while looking directly at Phil. "May we return?"

"Who is it?" Phil asked.

"One moment, please," Kimberley said into the phone. She punched the hold button and stood up. "Don't do that to me. It affects my credibility if I tell someone you're in a meeting and you interrupt me like that."

"Credibility?" Phil asked. "Who is it?"

"It's Steven Spielberg's business manager, back from Europe. He says some tax papers are still missing. Would you like me to take a message? I can do that."

"Is it necessary to use that tone of voice with me?" Phil asked.

"For what you're paying me," Kimberley replied, "you're lucky I use my voice at all. Do you want this call or not? I don't care."

"I'll take it," Phil said. "I'll take it in my office."

When Phil retreated, and I had a moment to myself, I realized that Bobby Savino's estimation of my chances of breaking into the business as a director was probably correct. Without having a real credit to my name or a property to hang my hat on, I had slim hopes of convincing anyone to take a chance on me. To make matters worse, I was broke. I worked in a rundown office on a street lined with T-shirt shops, drug paraphernalia stores, and lingerie boutiques. I couldn't even make a lunch date. Who was going to listen to me, anyway?

The morning after Bobby's visit, Phil called me into his office. "What do you think about this?" he asked. "The tortoise and the hare. There's a tortoise and a rabbit and everybody thinks the rabbit is going to win, but the rabbit gets distracted along the way and the tortoise emerges with the victory. First impression?"

"I like it," I said, following Phil's advice to answer without hesitation.

"Of course you like it," he said. "Underdog versus the system. Victory against all odds. But follow me on this: I have to give it a contemporary twist. I know that. Otherwise it has no meaning.

"The other day I read about a group of people going back to a kosher lifestyle. No meat with eggs. No, no, no. I mean no meat with the milk. Special plates at certain times of year. It's not for me, but I admit there's a feeling involved, a family feeling I find very attractive. You know about kosher, yes?"

I nodded. "You could do that if you wanted to," I suggested.

"Do what?"

"Become kosher."

"Hah, tell that to my wife. And what, I'm going to eat lunch by myself every day? What about Chinese?" Phil seemed distraught. He took a deep breath. "Isn't that funny? I just thought about Anne Frank, as if I had been there. What that family went through. Talk about pain. That was real pain."

Phil walked to the window and stood looking out. He mumbled a few words. I believe he was speaking Yiddish.

"Back to business," Phil continued when he'd collected himself. "Listen to me, Sheldon. No one remembers the beginning of a movie, not usually. It's the ending they remember. Although it's also true that no producer who knows what he's doing will read past the first five or ten pages of something he doesn't like. I should say if he or she doesn't like what he or she doesn't like.

"I want—whether it's a turtle literally or figuratively— to make a movie where our audience is on their feet cheering like it's fucking Rocky Balboa himself in the ring at the end. A character who's been knocked down so many times you just have to marvel he's still alive. And when he gets back on his feet . . . Christ, I got a chill down my spine. Could you feel it?"

I nodded.

"The problem is I've been so screwed up I've got everything backwards. What we've got to do, Sheldon, the two of us, is to round up some of these characters who have made money on Sandy's parking lots and get them to put their money into production. You'd think they'd be prime candidates, but then when it's time to invest in a movie nobody can find their checkbook."

Abruptly, Phil hit an automatic dial code. After saying a few words of Spanish on the phone to his maid, he stood up and left.

The door to the office was unlocked when I arrived the next morning. I was surprised to hear Phil whistling. "I think we've reached the turning point," he chimed in greeting. "Nothing but good things from here on out."

I noticed that several minor events, which ordinarily would have agitated Phil, did not seem to bother him at all. For example, when super-agent Larry Kibble had his secretary call to say that Larry had decided not to invest in a parking lot "at this time" because he was thinking about buying a beach house in Malibu and wanted to conserve cash, Phil didn't argue, even with the secretary. "It sounds like the right decision for Larry," Phil said. "Give him my best."

And when a new employee in Steven Spielberg's business manager's office mistakenly called requesting tax forms totally unrelated to the parking lots, Phil was patient, almost gentle.

"There's no reason to be discouraged," he told me several times.

Twice he sent me to the library for specific back issues of magazines.

"Does this mean anything to you?" he asked me after lunch. "'When Broadway was Broadway?'"

"It sounds like the title of a play," I said. "I don't know."

"It does, doesn't it?" Phil looked at his calendar and made a face. *"You make a reservation. I'll make a reservation. He made a reservation. This restaurant doesn't take reservations. I made a reservation, but they lost it.* Who am I?"

"You look like Phil Fried to me."

"You didn't get my impersonation?"

"Impersonation?"

"Yeah." He screwed up his face again. *"You make a reservation. I'll make a reservation. He made a reservation. This restaurant doesn't take reservations.* Who am I?

"I don't know," I said. "I'm sorry."

"You didn't get it?"

"I'm sorry, Phil."

"Then I'll tell you: I was impersonating Jackie Mason."

"Jackie Mason?"

"That's right. You don't know Jackie Mason?"

"I guess I've heard the name," I said.

"You guess you've heard the name?"

I nodded.

Phil smiled benevolently and took a deep breath. "I can't put my finger on it," he said. "I'm beginning to feel like myself again."

"That's great," I said.

For a few days it was almost fun.

A Year From *Shavuos*

I don't know if it was the unanswered phone calls. Or the abruptness with which Max Planck cut Phil off while I was sitting in his office. Or that Kimberley was out for a couple days because she got a few lines in a soap opera and had to say that someone in the office was finally working. Phil began to lose his composure over little things, like not being able to find the right size paper clips or his letter opener.

Phil confessed to me that he felt like a psychiatrist who loses a brilliant insight when he falls asleep after jerking off. I'm not sure what he meant, and I'm certainly not an expert, but I knew that something was wrong.

Phil told me that he had decided to concentrate on three story ideas. Since each was original, he was sure there would be no problem with the underlying rights involved. He said that when these stories were whipped into shape he was going to take them into the marketplace with a vengeance the industry had rarely seen.

The first idea involved a poor black woman who is introduced while waiting for a bus to take her home from work on Christmas Eve. An angel, visiting Earth, offers her a lift in a run-down car. The woman goes with her intuition, accepts the ride, and then a lot of wacky and wonderful things begin to happen. One aspect of the movie Phil described was that only this woman could hear the angel speak. Phil conceded this wrinkle was not "one-hundred-percent fresh," but thought it created some nice possibilities. First, he said, people like a holiday theme. Secondly, he asserted, we've all had some experience outside of normal reality that has affected us, often profoundly. Through the course of the movie, the woman gains a greater appreciation for the little things in life and in so doing shares a few laughs with the audience. Phil said that empathy for the main character would build right from the opening line when a bus that she hopes will be hers approaches only to bear an "Out of Service" sign. "'Out of Service' isn't me," she says to herself.

Phil's second story, "Ten Days at the Foot of the Buddha," concerned an obsessive businessman named Danny who runs his own company in the garment district of Manhattan. As the movie opens, Danny is forced to undergo a physical examination; he wants to take out a life insurance policy to protect his family. When the doctor and mobile check-up van arrive (great, Phil assured me, for a terrific visual moment and laugh because the van knocks over a fire hydrant), Danny must literally be dragged from his desk by his secretary and insurance agent. He leaves clutching two double chili-cheese burgers, a jumbo order of fries, and a chocolate milk shake.

The news is serious: Danny's blood pressure and cholesterol are out of control. His life insurance application is rejected. Danny consults his brother-in-law who happens also to be an internist. His brother-in-law explains that Danny is a "Type A" personality who, under the circumstances, must take a break. He posits several alternatives, including fat farms and 24-hour personal trainer services. The final choice is a meditation camp at a Northern California retreat site called Esalen. Although Danny balks at his alternatives, he ultimately decides to go to Esalen. "Why? Because I've been there," Phil said. "One hell of a location."

"Act 2," Phil continued. "Danny arrives at the meditation retreat and begins saying things like 'How much money did you make last year?' and 'This ten days is going to cost me so much I don't even want to know. Is that enlightenment?' Also, he becomes extremely upset when he can't find his slippers outside the meditation hall. And this happens fairly often because he is not wearing his glasses."

Phil suggested that there would be plenty of opportunities to work in fantasy scenes because of the many group and individual meditation periods during which it is necessary to interpose some kind of dramatic moment. "It's not enough to have them sitting there," he claimed. "You need something more. Let me give you an example. During one scene when each 'camper' is supposed to be focusing exclusively on the breath, Danny imagines that he is being chased through the desert by naked women riding horseback while a group of Indians whoops it up in the background. And things like that."

Phil thought that it would be funny if the more experienced meditators would have to struggle to get up in the morning due to the very early hour, but Danny would always be first to rise. And in spite of the rules requiring absolute silence, Danny would greet everyone at breakfast with a big "Good morning!" Then he would eat "like there's no tomorrow and say, 'Be here now!'"

Phil conceded he was going to need to develop an effective third act for his idea to appeal to people across the board. He thought the solution might lie in Danny's being able to offer something of spiritual value to the meditation teacher himself who by the end of the picture would become part of a very important experience in Danny's own life.

The third and last story, which Phil described as being "pure dynamite," concerned an undercover FBI investigation of corruption and race-fixing at a small East Coast racetrack. Hoping to attract a criminal element, two FBI agents assigned to penetrate this world intentionally purchase a horse with a mediocre record. To their surprise, the horse keeps improving—especially when Agent "A" is around.

Subplot as follows: Nothing in Agent A's life is working. He's going through a divorce, has serious financial problems, and in a moment which must be portrayed delicately so as to maintain the audience's sympathy, he confronts and overcomes an ethical temptation in relation to his job. In short, Agent A is down on his luck and drinks a lot of beer so that he won't feel like such a loser. The horse, however, seems to truly appreciate Agent A for himself and not because of the way he acts or because of any position he has been able to achieve. The horse continues to do well and the special relationship between the two flourishes. This helps Agent A turn things around in his own life, reconciling with his wife moments before their divorce papers are to be signed. Final scene: The President of the United States is rooting like crazy at Churchill Downs as our horse outruns the two favorites in a thrilling three horse ding-dong to win the Kentucky Derby. End credits over Agent A, wife, horse, and President in the winner's circle.

Phil didn't come in the next day. No phone call. No word from him at all. In spite of this, neither Kimberley

nor I were anxious to call his home. When later that afternoon we finally did, Mrs. Fried included the word
"episode" in her assessment of the situation. She told us
that Phil had been diagnosed as suffering from severe
exhaustion and would return to work only when his doctor felt confident that his new medication had taken hold.
Kimberley assured Mrs. Fried that we would take care of
things in the office. And that's what we did, eventually
creating shifts so that neither one of us had to waste time
if the other was going to be there.

During this period, on one of my expeditions around
the neighborhood, I was confronted again by a totally
unrelated mystery, something which had been confusing
me. To reiterate, Phil's office was not in the best part of
town. And yet, from time to time, I was sure I had seen
various celebrities in the vicinity of our building, and
inside, too—standing in the lobby or riding the elevator.
One afternoon, while browsing through magazines at a
nearby Thrifty Drug Store, I could have sworn I saw both
Bruce Willis and Chevy Chase buying cigarettes. I tried to
be as nonchalant as possible, but figuring there was nothing to lose I introduced myself and told them I worked
with Phil Fried—producer Phil Fried. They acted like real
gentlemen and recounted how each had struggled for
some time while waiting for a break. Appearances can be
misleading, but they seemed sincere. I liked the way they
wished me good luck.

I couldn't get over this, but when I mentioned my conversation to Kimberley she started laughing so hard I
thought that she was going to fall off her chair. "The third
floor," was all she could say.

So I went down to the third floor. Did I feel stupid.
There was a small talent agency in our building that handled celebrity look-alikes. On my way back to the

elevator, I passed Ronald Reagan and Michael Jackson debating about their favorite Mexican restaurants.

Following this revelation, I decided to make a more complete tour of our building. Even during regular business hours, almost half the doors were locked. I wasn't sure if this was for security purposes or if the tenants were out. Judging by the names on the doors, it was the usual assortment of businesses, including a wholesale jeweler, a market research firm, and a condominium time-share resort/travel agency. I knocked on a few doors to introduce myself. Most people knew Phil. Some didn't. One person asked me what movie we were working on. Another's response was, "Oh, yeah, the parking lots."

But the point I want to make is that this is how I met Christine. She sat behind the glass desk in the building's management office, perched perfectly on the edge of her chair for maximum effect in the micro-miniskirt she was wearing.

Still gun-shy from my experience with Rhonda in the camera store, I resolved to start slowly with Christine. I wanted to maintain control of the situation. Although Christine and I did speak for some time, I can't say that every aspect of our conversation was encouraging. When I referred to a novel I had read in college and enjoyed, her response was, "Fiction or non-fiction?"

While not rushing things might have been the right course with Rhonda, I could see that I would need to be more assertive with Christine. So I mentioned two or three times that I had access through my job to tickets to some interesting events. I figured that even if I had to buy them myself, it would be worth it. Christine appeared to be noncommittal in her response.

I paused for a moment in the hallway, then decided to go back inside to speak with her some more, try to firm up some plans for the weekend, if possible. Unfortunately, Christine must have left her desk during the very instant I was making up my mind. When she reappeared from her boss's office, I was standing in the reception area. "Can I help you?" she asked.

"I thought I forgot something," I said. "Maybe not."

Phil returned to the office on Friday. Apparently his medication had taken hold. He didn't say anything about his absence and neither did Kimberley nor I. In retrospect, I believe it was over the next few days that Phil and I ratified the unspoken pact we seemed to have formed with one another. The roots of this bond, I suspect, could be traced to the non-relationship Kimberley implied that Phil had with one son (doing post-graduate work at a medical school on the East Coast) and my own non-relationship with my father (doing his post-graduate work on an Ohio golf course). As far as I was concerned, Phil was free to lead the parade. As far as he was concerned, I was there to follow.

Phil was much calmer than I expected following his "episode." He took genuine delight in hearing news about an auto accident involving two executives he didn't like on one of the studio lots. Each man had simultaneously run a stop sign, the result being a ton of damage to the two late-model Mercedes they were driving. One executive was in charge of production. The other was in charge of marketing, so there may have been an underlying tension—even animosity—to begin with. It wasn't long before there were efforts to round up witnesses, some pushing and shoving, and a studio nurse called onto the scene to treat the marketing executive's bloody nose. One version of the story had the production executive rushing the marketing executive, screaming, "If you can't kill me one way, you try another!" The marketing executive, seemingly content to absorb the other man's largely ineffectual blows, nonetheless proudly paraded his bloody nose and handkerchief, and was reportedly first to utter the word "attorney."

"Max Planck saw the whole thing," Phil beamed.

Monday I had to have my own car towed into the shop. Being so close to the dawn of the third millennium, one would think a car should be able to run with air conditioning and not overheat. On the plus side, the young woman who came to pick me up in the tow truck was a knock-out. She helped me to conceive of an idea for a television pilot in which a single mother supports two children as a tow truck operator. Working title: "Maureen!"

When I did stumble into the office around noon, Phil wasn't there. He didn't come in the next day, either. Having just been through this, Kimberley and I decided to wait before calling Mrs. Fried. Being fully aware of the breadth of Phil's personal network—which made it possible for him to operate the way he did—but also recognizing the shallowness and lack of any meaningful prospects in his day-to-day activities, we were hardly concerned about covering for him. In fact, we felt as if we'd been granted yet another unscheduled holiday.

The next morning Kimberley handed me a note from Phil requesting that I deliver his mail, phone messages, and "any other relevant materials" to 1212 North Robertson, Suite 870.

"It was dropped off by messenger service," Kimberley said.

"No phone number?"

"Don't ask me. I just work here."

The address belonged to a hospital. My intuition upon entering was that Phil had lost it completely and was in for psychiatric evaluation. As the elevator lurched toward the eighth floor, I found myself thinking about a lot of things—not only Phil's recent happy period and his ridiculous story ideas, but about an incident that had occurred as well. Phil and I were sitting together at a booth in a coffee shop when he remembered a phone call that he needed to make. Neither one of us had two dimes or a quarter. Rather than stand in line behind several other customers to ask the cashier for change, Phil took some coins out of a charity appeal box sitting on the counter. After he made the call and we finished lunch, he put all the money back and then some, but I still thought it was a strange thing to do.

When the elevator stopped on the eighth floor, I was surprised to see that it was the orthopedic ward, not the psychiatric. I'm glad Phil wasn't in for psychiatric evaluation. God knows what they would have found.

Outside Phil's room I heard him instructing a nurse about how to adjust his pillow. "This way," he said at least three times. Although I knocked loudly, Phil did not respond until his nurse had gotten the hang of it. When I stepped into the room I think Phil smiled, but perhaps my entrance aggravated a facial nerve or else the nerve was already aggravated and I had imagined the smile.

My first reaction—I want to be honest—was that it made me happy to see that useless son-of-a-bitch lying helplessly in traction and in so much pain. Then Phil introduced me to the nurse he had been badgering. "This kid is going to be one hell of a filmmaker someday," he said.

There was a small shining part of Phil's personality that came through in the most unexpected moments, a part that said, *As long as I'm here, everything's going to be all right—even if it isn't now.*

My attitude changed completely. If I could have picked him up and carried him out of there I would have. If he'd asked me to, I certainly would have tried. Oddly, I felt a touch of regret; surely one day I would no longer run errands for this man. In that instant I wished I could work in Phil's office forever.

The nurse welcomed my arrival as her opportunity to go.

"I'm better," Phil told me. "If I could get this screw out of my leg, I'd jump out of bed and walk out of here."

"Do they know what it is?"

"It hurts," Phil said. "The doctor said I have a ruptured disk, but I think it's more serious. I feel like I've had a spinal collapse."

"Are they going to operate?"

"We don't know yet."

"What's with the screw in your leg?"

"There's nothing wrong with my leg, Sheldon. It *feels* as if there's a screw in my leg. The disk in my back is sitting on a nerve. The nerve is like an electric wire. It sends the pain all the way down to my toes. It's normal." He twitched. "I'm better. Let's see the mail."

As I watched the window envelopes flutter across his bed, I realized I had no idea a person could have so many credit cards.

"Those are from Sandy," Phil said, jerking his head toward the exquisite floral arrangement sitting on a small white table next to the window. "He can't get down here himself so he sends flowers. I'm better, though." He grimaced. "What's happening in the office?"

"No major developments," I said. "I wish I had something to report."

"We need some new customers. What have you been doing with your time?"

"The usual."

"The usual." Phil smiled. "Well, enjoy your vacation. We're going to be busy when I get back. P.S. I don't want anybody to know I'm in here. All right? NOBODY. Is that clear? Bring my mail and messages by every afternoon. Nobody! Is that clear? Nobody! *Capiche?*"

"*Capiche,*" I said. "Is there anything else you'd like me to do for you while you're in here?"

"Yeah, one thing," Phil said. "Don't do me any favors."

We laughed.

Life Goes On

My roommate during this period—indeed the entire time I lived in Los Angeles—was an aspiring screen-writer named Doug. He was extremely witty and showed lots of promise in the three or four pages he actually wrote. Mostly, he claimed, he was working things out in his head, which is not to say that he didn't like to talk. After a while, I had to ask Doug not to tell me about what he was working on until it was written down on paper. If this request irritated him, he seemed to bounce back quickly. Aggravating Doug was not something I wanted to do. Although I paid half the rent to sleep in the living room of our one bedroom apartment, I was glad to do so. There weren't many alternatives I could afford.

Doug and I tried to collaborate once on an idea I thought might make a good piece for the *LA Weekly*, a hip giveaway newspaper featuring articles on life in L.A. and specializing in advertisements for movies, concerts, record stores, plastic surgeons, and telephone sex lines. My idea was to describe the ten worst traffic intersections in the city. Doug agreed enthusiastically that this was a worthwhile topic. But it was hard to get him to sit down to work, and harder to get him to concentrate when he did. Out of frustration—and to show that the problem in our collaboration was not mine as he suggested—I finished the piece on my own and sent it off.

Doug and I were more effective as a team when creating a theoretical plan to provide privacy should either one of us get lucky on short notice and want to bring a girl home. I say "theoretical" because we never had to implement our scheme, which involved hanging a necktie on the apartment's front doorknob.

Doug kept a very strange schedule. He was usually asleep when I left for work in the morning. There was often evidence—dirty dishes in the kitchen sink, toothpaste in the bathroom sink—that he had been up during the day. But he was often asleep again (or waking up, or getting up and hogging the shower), when I arrived home from work at about seven or eight o'clock at night. Doug left his things lying around the apartment, like a membership card to a very expensive gym he never used. I'm still not sure about the source of his income. I suppose it came from his folks.

One thing about Doug really bothered me. He would start to invite himself to one of my few social events; then moments later, he would say he couldn't go. He would ask, "What are you doing tonight?" And I would say, "I'm going to a party."

"Whose party?"

"A guy named Rocco."

"Do I know him?"

"I don't think so."

"What time does the party start?"

"Nine."

"Can't make it."

Entering the lobby of our office building from Hollywood Boulevard one morning, I noticed John Travolta and Eddie Murphy look-alikes sharing a cigarette by the elevator. Immediately, I flashed on a super premise in which these stars could team in a buddy picture featuring two soldiers who overcome personality incompatibilities to work together for the common good.

Location: the Middle East. Mission: to incapacitate a ruthless tyrant. Title: "The Moses Affair."

Rather than on a battlefield, the climactic scene takes place at a discotheque on the French Riviera while the two men are on leave. To a medley of classic disco music, the pair duel with each other on the dance floor under a laser light show. First John, and then Eddie, struts his stuff in fabulous solo action. By the middle of the third act, it becomes clear that these two men are not only the best soldiers in the U.S. Army, but the best dancers as well. Although sparks fly along the way—over military dress, over women, over dance moves—the two are destined to become best friends.

I don't think that there can be any doubt Bobby Savino's suggestion that I needed to write something before I would ever be able to direct was working its effect in my subconscious.

Impulsively, I punched the sixth floor button in the elevator so I could visit Christine. It couldn't have been much past nine-thirty, but God help me if, when I opened the door to her office, she didn't have her head on her desk and she wasn't sound asleep. I left a short note close to her slightly open mouth, "Hello, from Sheldon."

Walking back to the elevator, I was inspired with another story: Chris cannot stay awake at work. He tries everything—coffee, donuts, more coffee, more donuts, naps during lunchtime, even calisthenics in the bathroom.

Nothing seems to work. Of course as soon as it's time to go home again, Chris is filled with energy. He's a maniac who energizes scenes like the ones in *Flashdance* where everyone feels so great after working all day at the steel mill. And when it's time to go to sleep at night Chris can't, so he has to go out again.

I was so excited about this idea that I turned around in my tracks, thinking I would leave Christine another note thanking her for the inspiration, telling her about this character I named Chris in her honor, and asking if she was free for dinner on Friday night. I thought we would have more fun if we didn't have to be at work by a certain time the next morning.

When I opened the door to her office again, I must have startled her. She appeared embarrassed that she had been sleeping and then confused by the first note I had left on her desk. When I asked her out for Friday night, she seemed flustered. "I have plans tonight."

"No," I said, "not tonight. Friday night."

She said, "I have plans on Friday night, too."

I comforted myself with a pat on the back for making the effort, but I felt extremely dejected. I have an informal guideline that if a girl turns me down for a date three times in a row, I refuse to ask her out again. And now, due to a silly misunderstanding, Christine had turned me down twice, once for that night and once for Friday night, too.

Howard Fingerman called me at home as I was climbing onto my sofa bed. "I've been invited to perform at The Laugh Club tomorrow night," he said. "You might note that's not a Monday."

"I think I know what day of the week it is without your help, Howard."

"You don't get it, do you?"

"Get what?"

"It's not amateur night!"

Howard explained that he was trying to get a "gang" together because if he had a good turnout the club was more likely to invite him back. He threw out several names of people who might attend. I heard one: "Madeline."

Howard also mentioned that he intended to leave Graphic Toner. He bragged that he had received several offers from traffic schools which employ comedians as instructors. Theoretically, their humor helps students bear the eight hours of class time required before a traffic citation can be removed from the California Department of Motor Vehicles's records.

Madeline didn't show at The Laugh Club. Although disappointed by her absence and irritated when people started disappearing after the waiter brought our check, I will admit that Howard was developing a decent routine. He began by discussing his experiences—imagined, I knew—of managing a fast-food restaurant. Responsible for the "Thank You" signs written on the trash receptacles at his college, he claimed that he had quickly advanced to become manager of the school cafeteria. A recommendation from his supervisor then led to a summer job at the local Dairy Queen, where he worked as assistant night manager, a position for which he was chosen over forty-six other candidates. Howard got his best response when he disparaged the tops of soft drink take-out containers that never seem to work properly. He also got some laughs when he talked about his tendency to eat too much of the leftover food at closing time. I don't think I'm doing justice to Howard's routine because, while describing his experiences in the fast-food business, Howard also asked members of the audience where they were from. In addition, he dealt effectively with one boisterous heckler and a drunk who knocked over a table just as Howard was establishing his rhythm. When the table and glasses came to a rest on the floor, Howard took the microphone in hand with authority and in public address-like fashion intoned, "Attention! Attention! Is there a designated driver in the house?" Applause erupted.

Howard segued confidently into a parody of the outgoing messages people leave on their answering machines. "'Please leave a message after the beep,'" he said. "Anyone who doesn't know what to do after the beep, raise your hand. I mean, *come on!*"

The final segment of Howard's performance included an overview of romantic relationships, a discussion about how screwed up his family was, and a rundown of what it's like to audition for a commercial. All this in ten minutes.

While getting drunk and watching Howard perform on stage, I thought about what could possibly motivate him to mock himself so desperately for a few laughs. I had a small insight that night. I began to understand that I had chosen a field which was not all glamour and approval. A lot of people involved in the entertainment arena weren't fun or wonderful at all. Many weren't even nice.

I received a letter from my mother saying that things were fine at home and wondering if everything was all right with me since they hadn't heard in a while. She also made the suggestion that I call a screenwriter named Peter

Yergin, the cousin of a friend of my mother's former tennis pro, whom she had run into at the post office.

Peter had only recently—after a number of years of trying—become a hot movie-of-the-week writer following enthusiastic response to his first two projects: a two-hour docudrama based on the life of Corazon Aquino titled "Mother, Leader, Woman," and another on the life of Abraham Lincoln titled "Father, Leader, Man."

I called, half expecting Peter to blow me off. Although we were interrupted several times by the call-waiting feature on his telephone, Peter quickly established that I was neither a competitor nor a benefactor. In spite of my lack of credentials, he graciously invited me to join him for a cappuccino the following Thursday afternoon, asking only that I confirm our plans the morning of our appointment.

I was fully prepared for Peter to cancel when I called to confirm. He didn't. We met without complication at a new coffee house the *LA Weekly* had been touting. Customers placed orders at a counter and carried their coffee back themselves. Peter was "a little low on cash" and hadn't had time to get to the automatic teller machine. Guess who paid.

"I've been working with Phil Fried," I said as we shuffled toward a tiny table in the back.

I don't think Peter was listening.

"Do you take Prozac?" he asked me.

"No."

"You might want to look into it. It's amazing what a different person I am these days."

I didn't know what to say. We sat down. "Do you think this table would stop wobbling if I put a couple sugar packets under one of its legs?" I asked.

"Let's talk about you," Peter said. "When I started out, I didn't have a clue as to how to begin. Whatever thoughts you may have to the contrary, this business is not about self-expression and it's not about innovation. If the toaster had been introduced in the entertainment industry, we'd all still be heating bread in the oven. Believe me, I know what I'm talking about. If I didn't, I wouldn't be making so much money.

"Realistically, you have one shot at getting into this business on a meaningful basis, whether your long-term goal is to write, direct, or produce. You have to write a great screenplay. If you don't have a writing background, take a screenwriting course. I recommend Don Blake's."

According to Peter, Don Blake was an instructor able to impart everything an aspiring screenwriter needed to know, particularly regarding the ins and outs of fundamental 3-Act structure. Blake would provide this enlightenment to anyone willing to pay the required tuition, attend class, and take close notes.

Although Peter did virtually all the talking, he seemed strangely sensitive when, out of some need to assert myself, I hesitated at his offer to get together again soon. "I'm just overwhelmed," I said, "by my responsibilities in the office combined with the efforts I've been making to get my own projects off the ground."

"What kind of projects?" he asked.

Mumble, mumble, mumble. I stammered and then fell silent. It seemed as if Peter could cut right through my bullshit. I felt irritated, too. Why should I have to pick up the tab for someone who was lording his success over me? With my car just out of the shop and my paycheck delayed because Phil was in the hospital and hadn't had a chance to sign it, money was tight. Real tight.

Cooped up in the apartment while Doug channel-surfed the TV, I found myself going stir-crazy. It was past midnight on a weeknight. I couldn't think of anything better to do, so I drove to my neighborhood Vons, a twenty-four hour supermarket. Walking in, I passed a group of people roughly my age buying cigarettes. They must have been out to a club together earlier. I noticed one of the women. She seemed different. I mean, she was dressed in black and wore dark makeup like the other two women in the group, but the get-up didn't seem as natural on her.

I angled over, edging closer to where she was studying the different kinds of chewing gum. I glanced at the magazines and newspapers next to the gum and candy display. One of the tabloids had a headline that read, "Chimp Test Proves IQ Of 120." I remember this clearly because I read it so many times before I could get up the nerve to ask her how she was doing.

"I could be better," she said.

"In what way?" I asked.

She considered my question for a moment before answering. "Every way."

Before I could say "boo" we were involved in a serious conversation. Even when her friends had purchased their cigarettes and were waiting for her by the door, she acted as if she didn't care. In particular, she seemed to ignore the one guy who was probably her boyfriend—at least he acted that way, semi-mopey and possessive.

We talked about what we did for a living, how much we hated Los Angeles, and what we hoped to accomplish in the future. She told me that her name was Carrie. She was working as a waitress, but had moved to Los Angeles from Seattle with one thing, and only one thing, in mind: "To really make it as a waitress."

Horrified by her misstatement, she stopped. "I mean," she resumed, "to really make it as an *actress*."

Carrie invited me to a cold reading/improvisation class held every Wednesday night, which she described as being more of a workshop run by actors for actors. She said that there was another director who sometimes sat in, and a writer who occasionally submitted scenes as well. She said that if I wanted to attend she was sure it would be all right and she told me where it was. As cynical as I'd become, I couldn't help but feel she really wanted me to be there.

So I went. Carrie was late, but everyone else made me feel welcome, especially the teacher, a guru for actors named Vincent. Vince, as he preferred to be called, talked about "getting to the heart of things" and "taking it to a whole new level by raising the stakes."

One by one, workshop members performed a variety of dramatic improvisations based on situations briefly described on a piece of paper. I enjoyed guessing how Vince would react to certain scenes. Sometimes I expected to hear praise because a scene was so entertaining, realistic, or just so much fun, but instead he would criticize it. Other times the scenes seemed to go overboard, change direction in a preposterous way, or ring utterly false, but Vince would rave about how beautifully the actors were "putting it out there, exploring dangerous new territory" and taking the kind of chances that would land them jobs.

About three quarters through the evening, Vince asked me if I wanted to do a scene. He handed me a piece of paper that read, "Three chickens, an onion and a bag of carrots."

"I've never done anything like this before," I said.

"Don't worry. It'll be good for you."

I suppose that paralysis is one form of assent. Fortunately, the brightness of the stage lights made it difficult for me to see the audience. I can't vouch for the quality of my performance. According to what one student told me later, I did stay in character. (Just *whose* character, I'm not sure.) I spoke about a peasant woman who appeared in a blinding deluge during a critical time of need and who fed a starving revolutionary army with provisions that included only three chickens, an onion, and a bag of carrots. As the scene progressed, something automatic took over. I described the beauty of this woman, who was unlike any woman I had ever seen. I concluded by yelling, "The days of '*Si, señor*,' are over!"

There was a lot of applause. Several people asked if this was really my first scene. Spontaneously, I gave Vince a big hug. I felt so exhilarated that it was difficult to pay attention to the next scene in which Carrie and an actor were improvising about how Christmas was ruined when the family dog was run over.

The whole group went out for pizza afterward. I asked Carrie for her phone number, which she released without too much resistance. I couched my true intentions with the suggestion it might be constructive if we rehearsed a couple scenes together that were included in a book I owned.

When I called her the next night, however, I decided to skip the bull about getting together to rehearse and instead asked her directly for a date. She responded positively, if not enthusiastically. It seemed too easy to be true.

Unfortunately, it was. Carrie was not where she was supposed to be at the time we agreed to meet. When I finally reached her three days later, she said that she hadn't shown up because her dog had gotten run over and she had to take it to the vet.

I had a hard time falling asleep that night. When I did, I dreamed that I was living in the year 2619. I remember even in the future I had no money. And I still couldn't get a date.

The next day at work I received a call from an editor at the *LA Weekly*. The piece I submitted about the ten worst intersections in Los Angeles had been accepted for publication. She asked me if I had taken any pictures and, when I said I hadn't, told me that she would assign a staff photographer. Finally, she asked me how I wanted to be identified.

After thinking for a moment, I said, "Sheldon Green is a writer-director who lives in Los Angeles."

"Got it."

Phil's New Office

Bobby Savino was sitting in Phil's hospital room when I entered.

"I didn't tell him that you're here," I said to Phil.

He laughed. "Sheldon, pour me a glass of water, would you?"

It may be necessary to understand the layout of that little room to comprehend how ridiculous a request this was. Bobby was seated next to the side table where the plastic pitcher and drinking cup were located. In order for me to get to the water I would literally have had to climb over him.

Sizing up the situation, Bobby lifted the pitcher. Watching him pour, I understood why Phil had asked me. Half the water in the pitcher must have spilled onto Bobby's pants, the table, and the floor.

"Just pretend that you're mixing a drink," Phil advised Bobby.

Then Phil turned to his favorite subject: the automobile accident on the studio lot. He insisted on repeating a joke that had been circulating. I remember because it was in such poor taste.

"What do you get when a yellow Mercedes and a red Mercedes collide on a studio lot?" he asked.

"I don't know," Bobby said.

"Orange Jews."

I winced. Bobby and Phil laughed.

These two men had a tremendous ability not to deal with things. For example, when the subject of Bobby's divorce came up, all of a sudden Bobby was wondering out loud how there can be enough material in a can of shaving cream to last four or five months, but a can of whipped cream, if used every day, runs out in less than a week.

As for Phil, when Bobby mentioned an old acquaintance of theirs—a man who committed suicide after going bankrupt—Phil diverted attention to the nurse who had entered the room to dole out his medication. "Look at the way she counts the pills," he said. "Isn't that great? I love the way that lady counts the pills."

Phil then spoke about how affronted he was by the "young people" he claimed were now in control of the business. He said that the younger generation today had grown up watching television, whereas his generation had spent its formative years reading books and therefore understood "story" much better. "It's gotten to the point I don't know where to take quality material anymore."

Bobby didn't seem to mind. "We had our chance. Let these kids have theirs."

"We had our chance," Phil said, "but we didn't take money out like they do today. We left ours in. These kids do nothing but take money out and they don't put anything back."

"You left yours in?" Bobby asked. "Where?"

Bobby's visit concluded with a discussion of Phil's medical condition. His doctor wanted to wait before committing to surgery. "What do you think?" Phil asked Bobby.

"If there's a chance to avoid an operation," Bobby said, "I would."

"And leave the underlying problem as it is?"

Bobby shrugged. "So have the operation. Do whatever you want." He left.

"You have the mail?" Phil asked me.

I did. We discussed a few things that I should keep an eye out for, specifically a couple phone messages and letters he was expecting. Otherwise we seemed to be balancing the fact that nothing important had happened during Phil's absence with the pretense that many things depended on his return before they could proceed.

With so little to do in the office, I found myself thinking continually about the article I had written for the *LA Weekly*. I wanted to tell the whole world about it. But other than Howard and Kimberley there weren't many people I knew who would care. I worried how Doug would react. I feared he might claim credit for his involvement.

My excitement grew when the editor called me to ask for my social security number. She had neglected to mention in our previous conversation that there would be some small compensation coming my way.

I took the news as an especially good omen, perhaps the encouragement I needed to review my goals with a greater degree of honesty. For the first time, I was able to admit to myself that the grounds upon which I had originally decided to become a director were shaky. Growing up, I didn't know what I wanted to be. When people asked about my future, I would answer that I intended to become a director because I knew I didn't want to be a doctor or a lawyer and I couldn't think of anything else.

When, as a high school student, I declared that I wanted to be a feature film director, the skeptics (meaning members of my family) may have laughed, but what could they say? After all, who wouldn't want to be a motion picture director?

I do know that even at a young age, I was hoping for a fresh start. And what I imagined about California and the entertainment industry fueled this fantasy as well as anything. How was I supposed to know that so many other people my age were thinking the same thing?

There is no doubt that the boost that came with landing an entertainment-related job represented an enormous step forward. And perhaps from an objective perspective my progress was obvious all the time. Still, on an emotional level, I felt more or less in the same place I'd been when I walked into the office of Graphic Toner: nowhere. So in spite of whatever headway I might have been making when I thought about my chances those days, I don't think I would have said they looked good.

My reassessment prompted one other thought. I had never considered myself a writer, but I was able to recall that when the screenwriter for my eight-minute college film project came down with mononucleosis, I wrote the key scene myself:

FIRST BROTHER
Hey, you guys, don't talk that way about Mom!

SECOND BROTHER
Mom? Who are you calling Mom? She's not your mom. You were adopted.

FIRST BROTHER
(shocked)
Oh, my God. I need to sit down.

The problem was that I never felt like writing. I had to motivate myself by thinking about money or what writing could do for my career. And even then, I preferred coming up with ideas for things I would write another time. Sometimes when tired, I even found myself watching television with Doug rather than sitting down to write as I had promised myself I would. When I tried to work first thing in the morning it was worse. Nothing would come out at all.

After suffering as much of this frustration as I could bear, I did two things. First, I got more information about the screenwriting course Peter recommended. Ouch, that was a lot of money to pay an instructor who had sold only two television movies himself. Second, I promised myself that, no matter what, I would write a screenplay within the next six months.

I did attempt an experiment when Doug wasn't around. With music playing softly in the background, I tried to ease myself into a semi-hypnotic trance. Not pressuring myself to do anything other than take a few notes, I felt my creative juices flowing. To my astonishment, all sorts of incidents from the time I spent at Graphic Toner burst forward, almost insisting that they be worked into my screenplay idea about the character named Chris who will try anything to stay awake at work. In as relaxed a state of mind as possible, I reflected on my experiences at Graphic Toner and my recurring struggle with the temptation to eat all the donuts on the table by the coffee machine. I don't like coffee. I don't like donuts . . .

. . . but seeing what time it was, and thinking about how I was going to pass the rest of the day, I would feel tired and sense the need for something to fill me up. Sometimes I would consider the bigger picture—my health and things like that—but then before I knew what I was doing I was eating a donut, and one

donut often led to another. In fact, it bothered me that people who didn't think donuts were as bad for their health as I did were so much more disciplined than I was. And somehow even the thought that not all the donuts had been eaten made me anxious. Or that nobody cared how many I was eating. Donuts. Donuts. Donuts. Soon I was acting as if it was my mission to finish all of the donuts. From that first moment when someone would say the coffee was ready—or maybe nobody said it, I just saw that it was so—I would study the big container of artificial non-dairy creamer and think about how cruddy it was. Then I would look at the sugar and think about how hyper sugar makes me. I would see the pink paper packets of artificial sweetener and think about how much I hated the taste. I would see the box of donuts lying open nearby and there would be ten or eleven donuts inside and I would resolve to make it through the day without having even one. Then I would see somebody walk over to the table and I would be so lonely and bored that I would wander over too, first to prepare a cup of coffee with non-dairy creamer and sugar and then to pick up a donut. I don't eat the donuts because they look good. They don't; they look bad. I have a donut because the box is not getting any fresher and there's a lot of time left in the day. I have another, and perhaps there are only seven left. And even before it is close to noon, I say to hell with it and have another. Then since somebody else has had one or two, I am at my most vulnerable. There may be only a few left in the box. If someone doesn't eat them, they might be thrown away. Why not have a half? I ask myself. And then, I think, I might as well finish them all. Tomorrow is another day; I'll go cold-turkey then. When I've eaten the last one, I tidy up around the table and throw the gray cardboard box into the trash. I don't want to see the evidence or think about what I've done. I promise myself I will eat better in the future, but since I feel guilty about having eaten all the donuts today, I bring in a new box tomorrow. Donuts. Donuts. Donuts. Seven, six, five, four, three, two . . .

My trance-like state proved so successful that several times I believed myself to be the vehicle through which an important story could be told.

The first scene: Ted (I changed the main character's name from Chris to Ted so I wouldn't obsess as much about Christine) enters his office. He deals with computers, so there is lots of high tech equipment in the background. Ted walks in and somebody says, "Good morning." Ted notices a couple of associates in the corner having coffee and donuts and he ambles over. Everything is fine and he's still in control, but as the opening credits roll, we suspect that something is wrong with Ted because he sneaks back for a second, third, and fourth donut. The scene is capped when one of the secretaries, who has just finished telling another secretary about how she's trying to maintain her diet, makes a break for the coffee table, only to discover—to her ultimate relief—that the donuts she was craving are all gone. No dialogue is needed; we can tell how surprised she is by the look on her face.

With my mind racing, I slapped an outline into place. The first act relates the many strategies Ted employs to stay awake at work and introduces the problems this dilemma creates in his personal life. It also shows his growing desperation. At one point, Ted stumbles into the men's room, desperate to take a nap. Ted's supervisor notices his predicament. Instead of making the boss a heavy, I create a more interesting character by having his supervisor empathize, not criticize. When the supervisor fully understands our protagonist's affliction, the two sit down for a tête-à-tête. The supervisor discloses that he, too, once had the same problem. (It occurred to me that it might be a nice twist if the boss was a woman, although this would complicate the discovery of Ted napping in the men's room unless she storms in there herself out of frustration with her delinquent employee. An unnecessary risk?) The supervisor encourages Ted to rediscover what truly inspires him and build on that as a starting point from which to make a fresh start. If self-help does not do the trick, the company now employs a counselor to assist its employees with their personal problems. Eventually, Ted does meet with the counselor, and we have another enormously funny scene in which no dialogue is necessary: Ted's therapist nods off, head slumped forward onto a desk next to coffee mug, napkin, and half-eaten donut!

The telephone rang, startling me. It was Howard. "I need a collaborator," he said. "I have an idea that could be worth a lot of money and I like what you did with your article on the intersections."

Howard explained that thanks to the preponderance of comedian's routines about food, he had become aware of how many people are obsessed with what they eat. (If I'd been able to get a word in edgewise, I would have told him about my donut screenplay.) Howard said that he wanted to write a diet book and that he'd done some research at his neighborhood Crown Books. He claimed that the best-sellers all had catchy titles. This must be the key to their popularity, he speculated, because the contents were so similar: Common Sense + Will Power = Success. Howard would allow me to use the title he had conceived, "To Live And Diet At The Same Time," if I would write the book. He proposed that we split the profits fifty-fifty.

"I'll think about it," I said.

"Well, think fast. And don't tell anybody about our conversation."

"Don't worry about that."

When I hung up, I seemed to have lost my momentum entirely. I reviewed my notes and outline. It all looked like crap. I couldn't pretend. It was nothing but crap, crap, crap, and more crap.

Driving into work the next morning, I found myself wondering about what kind of place Los Angeles had been before there were automobiles and roads, before there were computers, paperwork, and insurance, before there were police. When it was a semi-arid rolling desert by the ocean with a scrub type of flora, when there were still deer in the hills.

I thought about what it was like to live in Los Angeles now. The air was unhealthful. People drank bottled water because the tap water smelled so foul. It wasn't safe to walk alone in most neighborhoods at night. Even with a car, it was a fight to get from one place to another. And yet, had I wanted to, I was nowhere near able to afford a house because so many people wanted to live in the city.

The truth is it wasn't the donuts, my car, the drinking water, or the smog. I felt lost and confused. And for the first time I could remember, I wanted to go home.

The Iris

I don't know what kind of drugs they were giving Phil. He was on medication even before he checked into the hospital, maybe it was the mix. The next time I saw him, he went off on any number of tangents. Among other things, he told me that he wished he'd gone into the pool-cleaning business. "It's a nice way to make a living," he said. "You're outdoors. You'd be surprised how much work there is, too."

Phil told me that he and Richard Pryor had invented the mooning gag. He also said that they had invented the modern form of the screwball comedy. I was treated to a number of stories like these while his doctor was playing it safe, taking time before deciding whether to operate.

I confess that when Phil was not fully conscious or able to understand what I was saying, I enjoyed needling him. I would ask him questions such as, "Have you heard of a company called Morgan Creek?" and "How does it relate to the bottom line?"

Phil is a guy who can handle himself pretty well, even on automatic pilot. When I asked him about the bottom line, he responded, "What has that got to do with us?" And when I asked about Morgan Creek, he replied, "We know they're serious, but we won't know until they make an offer whether they can be taken seriously."

When more fully coherent, Phil liked to complain about how he hadn't heard from anyone, and wasn't it just like his friends to abandon him when he was down? Maybe Phil's friends would have deserted him, I don't know. But since Phil insisted that nobody know where he was, I would hardly consider his friends' absence to be a fair test of loyalty. Other than his wife, who preferred to visit at night, myself, Kimberley, Bobby Savino, and brother Sandy—who never showed, but had the floral arrangement changed every fourth day—I'm not sure anyone knew that Phil was in the hospital.

Phil combed through *Variety* and *The Hollywood Reporter* to see if either included anything about his condition. "I always felt at least I have my health," he liked to say.

The end of his third week in the hospital brought a different kind of pain to Phil's face: he was bored. I was in the room when he called for a meeting with a hospital administrator to pressure his doctor into either operating on him or releasing him. The administrator told Phil that he had seen his doctor wait out situations with patients in far worse condition than he was in, and added that his doctor had mentioned only the day before that Phil was improving.

"I'm not sure you understand," Phil said to the administrator. "I want a decision now." He turned to me. "What do you think?"

"I think I'd listen to the doctor."

"All right," Phil said. "We'll wait."

The meeting broke.

A few days later, I completely forgot that Kimberley was going to be out for an audition. When I arrived in the office, there was a message on the answering machine left by Max Planck's secretary, asking Phil to meet Max at The Iris at twelve-thirty. The Iris is an industry restaurant and watering hole best known for its ability to do business with an unlisted telephone number.

Since it was already a quarter to eleven, I immediately called Max Planck's office.

"Mr. Planck is not in right now," his secretary said. "Would you like to leave a message?"

"No," I said quickly and hung up.

I rushed to the hospital. It was nearly eleven-thirty when I breathlessly walked into Phil's room. He was watching "Hollywood Squares" on television, criticizing the celebrities' responses.

I explained to Phil that I didn't know what to do because Max Planck was unavailable and The Iris's phone number is unlisted.

"You did the right thing," he said, flashing a mischievous smile. "Let's go."

"Phil, you can't," I protested. "There will be plenty of other opportunities." He had only started walking from his bed to the bathroom the day before.

"We're going," he said.

"Phil, think about what you're saying. There's no way."

He looked me in the eye. "Max Planck is in the right business for us."

"What business is that?"

Phil reached for the remote control lying by the side of his head and turned off the TV. "Max Planck turns shit into gold." He started to climb out of bed.

"What you're doing is outrageous," I said. "I'm not going to participate."

"Have it your way. You're fired."

"Phil, seriously, think about it."

"Listen to me carefully, Sheldon, and maybe you'll understand. There are roughly a hundred people in this town who can get a movie made at any given time. Among that group, Max Planck is the only one who's talking to me."

"You're sure you want to do this?"

"I'm sure."

"I'll help you."

"You'll help me? Didn't I just say you're fired?"

"Phil," I said, "I'll help you!"

"We need to get dressed."

I hesitated. Phil tried to lift himself and collapsed face down on his bed.

"It's my fucking life," Phil yelled into his pillow. "I can screw it up if I want to."

There wasn't much in Phil's closet, basically the clothes he wore when he arrived and a few things his wife had brought over. I virtually had to carry Phil from his bed to the closet to the bathroom mirror, so little weight could he put down on one foot.

There is no doubt the effort seemed to rejuvenate his spirits. He especially enjoyed telling me how I should cover for him when his nurse arrived to give him a sponge bath. "She doesn't want to do it," he whispered. "So tell her I've had one already and say, 'Thank you.' She won't argue."

She didn't.

What Phil did in that twenty minutes reminded me of my improvisation in Vince's Wednesday-night acting class: getting three chickens, an onion, and a bag of carrots to feed an army. Phil pulled himself together mostly on the basis of a pocket comb, a little baby powder, and a red paisley scarf. "How do I look?" he asked.

"You look like a cross between Frank Sinatra, Dracula, and the rabbi who performed my Bar Mitzvah," I said.

Phil chuckled. "Bobby Savino should hear that. Anyway, I'll take it as a compliment. But I don't feel as good as Dracula. Here . . ." He pointed to the lone sports coat and tie hanging in the closet. "Put those on. You look terrible."

"Thanks." Together with the worn corduroys and tennis shoes I was wearing, my outfit became so ridiculous I think I was almost fashionable.

"Let's get out of here," Phil said.

"Do we need anything else?"

"The pills. Take the pills."

I walked over to the night table. "Which ones?"

"All of them."

Holding tight to my right elbow, Phil hobbled to the elevator. Along the way, he grabbed an unattended aluminum walking cane. "Just in case . . ." he said.

When the elevator doors closed, Phil chattered nervously about how he had been hounding Max Planck for an opportunity to present some new ideas and that Max had been too busy to see him. Now that he was going to have a chance, Phil feared he was in no shape to make his bid.

He checked his watch to see if we had time to stop by the office. We didn't. Phil became concerned that his Rolex wasn't working properly. I couldn't help him with the correct time because I don't wear a watch. Phil didn't trust the clock hanging on the wall in the lobby because many years before a similar one had been off by fifteen minutes when his son had his tonsils removed.

I spotted a wheelchair and retrieved it so Phil could sit down. Then I wheeled him out of the building.

An orderly approached. Phil raised a hand. "It's all right," he said. "My doctor knows."

After some trial and error on the sidewalk, I was able to lock the wheelchair into a fixed position. I made a run for my car.

When I pulled up at the curb a few minutes later, Phil was about twenty feet down the street, his wheelchair resting against the trunk of a palm tree.

But Phil didn't complain, at least not at first. He did say I should get the clock on my dashboard fixed. I also got a lecture about the importance of proper support for the lower back, especially in a car seat. The way Phil was squeezing the door handle, it wasn't difficult to guess that he was in a lot of pain.

"I don't want anyone to see us in this car," he said as we approached the Iris. "And I don't mean that as a criticism. If we had more time we would have rented a car, but we didn't. We'll park on the street. We're not using the valet."

I circled the block several times before a muffler-less Plymouth Barracuda roared out of a parking space just around the corner. "Don't lose that spot!" Phil ordered over the noise.

I remain awed by whatever it was that allowed Phil to sashay through The Iris the way he did that day. Twice, he raised his cane in salute to people he knew at other tables. Once, when a waiter backed into him, the same Phil Fried who couldn't stand to have a nurse adjust his pillow improperly, smiled graciously and toddled along.

Max Planck was seated with a young man wearing a three-piece business suit at a prime location in the back of the restaurant. Max gave Phil's cane a long look, but continued with his story as Phil and I sat down.

"An American production manager," Max repeated for our benefit, "whom I took to England told me that he didn't see why it was necessary to adapt to foreign ways. 'Why don't you go for a drive,' I asked him, 'on the right side of the street?' Right side—that's the wrong side!"

Max introduced us to Ethan Albright by name only, promising to tell us more about him later.

Phil introduced me by first and last name too, adding almost as an afterthought that I was a future Academy Award-winning director temporarily lodging in his office.

"Sheldon Green," Max Planck considered the words carefully. "That's not a director's name. That name belongs to a writer."

There was a slight pause. Ethan mentioned he heard it might rain.

"Did they say it's going to rain?" Phil asked.

"There's a percentage," Max replied.

While things were still pretty much on the casual side, I feared that Phil began to compensate for his physical discomfort by talking too much. I say this because several times I felt that Max Planck was trying to speak to me. Not only had he raised no objection to my presence, but he seemed genuinely interested in my background—how long I had worked with Phil, what I had done before, and how I enjoyed college. I'm smart enough to know that "seemed" is the word that must be stressed, but it seemed that Max Planck was actually listening to what I was saying. And yet Phil kept interrupting in order to answer Max's questions himself.

"The thing I like about you, Fried," Max Planck said finally, "is that when I ask you a question directly I can never get a straight response. But if I ask someone else, you always have the answer."

Max's comment seemed to help the group relax. Phil gave me a light whack on the head. I thought about throwing his pills onto the table.

It turned out that Ethan Albright was a Harvard MBA who had completed a two year stint selling American assets to foreign clients for one of Wall Street's most respected firms. He was presently in Los Angeles on behalf of a large Japanese corporation that wanted to get involved in American motion picture production. As I would later understand, Max had enough experience to know that this lunch was probably a waste of time. He was bringing Phil into the equation as someone who knew what to do if anything developed, someone desperate enough to try. Ethan assured Max this was not a lark and that his investors were extremely serious about getting involved quickly. However, there is no doubt in my mind that if Max actually felt that day at The Iris he did have a bankable idea, property, screenplay, or other money-making possibility of his own, he would not have let Ethan know. On the chance that something might develop through Phil, Max would still be involved by virtue of having set the whole thing up, not to mention the larger distribution deal he would undoubtedly godfather.

We talked about many unimportant things over lunch. Max told a number of jokes. Some were funny, some weren't. One concerned a businessman who meets an important supplier at the end of the year. "How's business?" the supplier asks. "Great," the businessman says. "Yeah, great," his supplier replies. "Last year you owed me a million dollars. This year you owe me two million."

I imagine Ethan felt compelled to respond. "That's funny," he said. "One of the first things we tackled in business school was cash flow. Most people have no idea how important it is to have more coming in than there is going out, even on a short-term basis."

"You went to business school to learn that?" Phil asked. He wiped an unused spoon with his napkin and shook his head. "By the way, what's the exchange rate with Japan these days?"

"It's good," Max answered. He turned my way. "What's breaking, son? What's in?"

"MTV," Phil replied. "MTV is very popular."

"Hitler was popular," Max snapped. "I'm not interested in popular. I want to know what's breaking so we can get there before it becomes popular."

After we ordered, Max pulled out a couple tickets to that evening's Laker game. He claimed the two floor seats had been forced upon him earlier in the day in spite of his protests that he would not be able to use them. Max asked Ethan if he wanted to go. Ethan said that he had a dinner engagement. Phil declined with a nod to his cane. And so they fell to me.

I feared that our lunch would go on forever and we would never get down to the real proposition. However, during what may have been no more than a three minute interval, initiated when the busboy cleared our main course dishes and concluded when our waiter arrived with the dessert tray, Max stated that the purpose of lunch was to introduce us—very kindly, I thought, he included me with Phil—to Ethan because he knew we had a lot of material "in development."

Ethan explained that his people hoped to make a family-oriented movie with international appeal. He quickly added that anything likely to make money would be considered.

Phil nodded vigorously.

Ethan declared it was not necessary for the movie to include a Japanese subplot or tie-in, and said he would personally prefer to recommend a project that was not dependent on special effects or a "name" star, both of which would likely inflate the budget. "Foreign investors have made a lot of mistakes in Hollywood," he said. "I need to protect my people."

"Domestic investors have made a lot of mistakes, too," Max replied.

Phil stopped nodding.

Business cards were exchanged—at least Ethan's was. Phil wasn't carrying his. I didn't have any. We agreed to meet again in a week or two.

Max Planck picked up the check over a mild protest from Ethan. I enjoyed seeing someone who could afford to pay actually do so. We adjourned following a brief discussion about the difference between Hawaiian papaya, as had been sliced and served alongside the piece of chocolate cake I was eating, and the papaya that comes from the Philippines, Indonesia, or Taiwan, which Ethan claimed was superior. Ethan was a papaya expert.

"I'm sorry, sir," the waiter said to Ethan after confirming with the kitchen that the origin of my papaya was Hawaii. "This is the only papaya we have."

"What's with the cane?" Max asked Phil when we were out on the street.

"My doctor told me I have to use it for a couple weeks."

"I wished I'd known," Max said as his car pulled up. "You could have borrowed mine."

Phil made sure that we stood outside the restaurant until Ethan was safely down the road before he would let me run around the corner to retrieve my dirty compact.

When I pulled up in front of the restaurant, I left the engine running and popped out of the driver's side to shoehorn Phil in. All of a sudden, he wasn't looking so good. I drove to the hospital as quickly as I could.

To my surprise, the wheelchair we abandoned on the street was still resting against the palm tree.

Wheeling Phil through the lobby, we waved to the same orderly who had questioned us as we were leaving earlier. "We're back," Phil said.

Up in the room, Phil's wife was waiting with their three year-old daughter. "How's my little girl?" Phil asked.

"Who are you speaking to?" his wife replied. Her smile was as fresh as Las Vegas. "Don't you ever leave the hospital without telling me where you're going!"

Phil collapsed onto his hospital bed. "Christ," he said before passing out, "do we need a hit."

A Big Break

That afternoon I enrolled in Don Blake's screenwriting course. It was a lot of money to spend and I felt open to criticism from Doug about subscribing to a "paint by the numbers" approach to the creative process. I was told by Don Blake's personal assistant that as soon as my check arrived I would be sent a packet of preparatory materials that I should be sure to review before the first class meeting. I was also informed that there would be no refunds.

My next task was to ask Christine to the Laker game. I decided to ask Kimberley for her advice on the best way to go about it. She was always talking about these things with her friends on the telephone. Why not take advantage?

"That little thing on the sixth floor?" Kimberley said.

"She's not that little."

"I'm sorry. Well, just go into Phil's office, close the door, and call. Apologize for such short notice and say, 'These tickets—probably on the floor, but I haven't had a chance to check—just fell into my lap. If by chance you're free, I would love to take you to the game.'"

And so I did what Kimberley said—with one exception. Instead of calling Christine as planned, I called Rhonda in the camera store. She didn't recognize who I was at first and when she did, she laughed at my invitation.

"Bye," I said and hung up. Although I felt like an idiot, I reminded myself that no one else need ever know. So I picked up the phone and called Christine.

Following Kimberley's advice to the letter, Christine actually indicated that she'd like to go to the game, but had to check her date book first. It seemed to take forever before she could find her calendar and confirm that she was free.

I had my first real lunch meeting, had enrolled in a class that would teach me how to write a screenplay, and had a date for the Laker game with seats right on the floor. I thanked Kimberley for her help and we embraced, which I think came as a surprise to both of us.

The basketball game was a disappointment. The Lakers went out to a big lead, lost it, then came back to finish strong. That wasn't the problem. The problem was that Christine wasn't into it. She kept yawning. During a time-out at the peak of the Lakers' fourth-quarter surge, I stood and sang "I Love L.A." along with the Laker Girls and 17,503 other enthusiastic fans. Christine had excused herself to the ladies room.

It must have taken us an hour to get out of the parking lot. No wonder so many people left early. Worrying the entire time that my car might overheat, I made a mental note to ask for a parking pass the next time I was given tickets—if there was a next time.

By the time we got out of there it was so late that neither one of us felt like going for a bite to eat. Then when it came time to drop Christine off, I couldn't take her home because her car was still at the office. I tried to drop a hint about being able to stop by my place, but she either pretended not to or just didn't pick up on what I was saying. I didn't push it. We finished the evening talking about how great it was that she could have one of the few parking spaces right in the building. We agreed that this was a benefit that comes with working for the office in charge of those things. Christine told me that she was going to visit her parents in Oceanside the following weekend. The way she said it seemed calculated to preclude any chance I had to ask her out on a second date as yet. What a great way to end the evening, I thought.

Phil was released from the hospital about a week later. He started in to the office again with half days, despite his doctor's instructions to stay home for at least another week. Although Phil had managed to avoid surgery, he looked as beaten up as if he'd had an operation performed without anesthesia.

"Life is too short," he told me on his first day back. "A person needs a minimum of two lives, or one life without all the shit."

Given how enthusiastic Phil was during our lunch at The Iris, I was surprised how little interest he now showed in Ethan's project. Phil claimed that he had been involved with this kind of thing many times in the past and that it had always been a waste of time. "Consider it a favor for Max Planck," he said. "When the time comes we'll trot out the old dog-and-pony show."

When I saw some of the material he was thinking about forwarding to Ethan's office, I couldn't believe it. One of the sheets in particular had a bluish tint and that distinctive smell—I mean it looked as if it had been run off a mimeograph machine.

I could hardly get Phil's attention at all that week. The only subject he wanted to talk about was his stay in the hospital. "It's a good thing I was really sick," I overheard him tell a neighboring tenant one morning in the men's room. "Or they would have killed me."

"Phil," I said, "do you remember you once told Bobby Savino you wished you had the phone number of a foreign producer who paid way too much for a screenplay?"

He looked at me blankly.

"Ethan has that phone number!"

"Sit down, Sheldon," he said. "I know you're enthusiastic. That's good. Don't lose your enthusiasm. That's not what I want. But trust me, it just ain't going to happen. This is a doomed enterprise you're talking about. There's no way."

I almost went crazy. "If you don't think it's worthwhile in itself," I asked, "why don't you think of it as a way to strengthen our relationship with Max Planck?"

"I don't have time for that kind of thing anymore. Look, if it means that much to you, why don't you do it?"

"Do what?"

"Put a presentation together."

"You want me to put a presentation together?"

"Yes."

"You don't mind?"

"Why should I mind? You're doing me a favor, right?"

"You're sure?"

"Yes."

"What kind of presentation do you want?"

"It's up to you."

"I can't believe it."

"What?"

"I'm going to work hard on this, Phil."

"Good. Let's at least get a few meals out of it."

I spent most of the next few days reviewing the jumble of screenplays lying around the office. I made some phone calls regarding the scripts I liked best to confirm their availability. I also called two or three working screenwriters I had spoken to about Sandy's parking lots. Unfortunately, they were unwilling to discuss their current speculative projects without receiving more information than I was willing to give.

I compiled a list of every worthwhile idea I had come across since I started working in Phil's office. I chose not to include my own idea regarding the man who cannot stay awake on the job because, as hard as I tried, I had no clue as to how it should end. I also did not list "The Moses Affair," remembering that Ethan preferred not to rely on a star and "Moses" needed two. For some reason, Phil would not give me permission to use his FBI-at-the-race-track/Agent "A" story line. I did, however, add one new idea of my own. Although still in its formative stages, I felt confident that this story—as yet told to no one—would represent my best shot.

In our first meeting, Don Blake asked me to stand in front of the other screenwriting students and pitch a movie premise based on the written material each of us had received in the mail. My gut instinct told me that, in an industry that produces only five-hundred-and-fifty feature films a year, a class of forty beginning screenwriters is necessarily going to represent more desire than talent. Refusing to take a chance on anyone stealing the idea I really did believe in, I pitched the least commercial concept I could imagine. I called it "To Really Make A Difference." It was the story of a surfer who retires from competition to organize his buddies into lobbying their surf association for life insurance benefits.

"What does your protagonist really want?" Blake asked me when I finished. *"Whole life or term?"* He went on to say that "To Really Make A Difference" was the worst idea he had heard in the fourteen years he had been teaching the class. "I assume you know how to read?" he asked.

"Yes," I said.

"And you received the preparatory materials from my office?"

"Yes."

"Did you read them?"

"Yes, I did."

"Right-side up?"

There was a lot of snickering when Don said this, particularly from a cliquish group sitting up front whose ringleader was a girl named Susan.

In fact, I had read the preparatory materials thoroughly. I also paid rapt attention to every spoken word in class and studied closely each of the many handouts. I was well aware of the sanctity, importance, and power of fundamental three-act structure. I was also familiar with the five genres, six necessary traits an interesting main character will have, seven questions a writer must ask himself, and twenty-eight building blocks which lead to box office success. I learned that when a screenplay is being discussed it is never a mistake to invoke the name Joseph Campbell. All this from an instructor who considered *Tootsie* and *Private Benjamin* two of the ten best movies ever produced.

"A movie is made three times," Blake proclaimed. "Once when it's written, once when it's shot, and once when it's edited. But if it isn't written well, it will never be shot. And if it isn't shot, it's not going to be edited. So when you sit down in front of your typewriters, computers, and word processors I want you to think about this: 'In the beginning was the word.'"

I confess I strayed from Blake's guidelines in developing my own favorite story. Perhaps the opportunity to read so many screenplays in Phil's office bolstered my confidence and gave me the courage I needed to proceed. Certainly I had been thinking about the market. I seemed to see it so clearly: the public was hungry for a movie Mom and Dad could take the whole family to watch without having to contend with a lot of complaining from the kids. And without anyone having to think too much. That my screenplay should be a comedy, I felt, was a given. The themes should feel fairly familiar without being a total rehash. In deference to Ethan, I was intent on avoiding the need for special effects or a star. If we could create a star, so much the better.

There is a certain part of the process I experienced which is difficult to describe. Let me simply say that there was an instant in which I saw the whole thing. Fortunately, I had placed a pen and paper next to my sofa bed. I was thus able to jot down the basics so that when I awoke the next morning it was all there.

My story was basically as follows. A chimp trained to get along with humans escapes from the circus and happens into the home of a middle-class family that has shipped one of its children overseas on an exchange program and is expecting a foreign student in return. Due to a bureaucratic mix-up, the parents of the family are not informed that the foreign exchange student has been delayed for eight weeks, so when they learn that a visitor has arrived at their house, they mistakenly assume that it must be Mitch, the exchange student. Because the two children still at home are only too willing to encourage this misunderstanding and because both parents are too caught up in their own lives to notice what their children are doing and because the chimp is accustomed to being around people and because everyone expects Mitch to be a little strange, the mix-up goes undiscovered for some time.

Aided by Mitch's winning personality, the children are able to keep their parents from figuring out that their guest is not who they think he is. Dad works the night shift at an auto parts manufacturer. If he is not at work or sleeping, he's too exhausted to pay attention to his kids. Mom's application for a part-time job has just been accepted at McDonald's, so she's not around the house much either. Dad actually comments about how much more peaceful it is to have Mitch around the house than his own son—in spite of the fact that Mitch plays drums, too!

I imagined lots of cute scenes featuring Mitch at the dinner table, Mitch clowning around in class, and the oh-so-popular Mitch escorting one of the high school cheerleaders to the prom.

I rushed to the library to learn everything I could about chimpanzees. I wanted my movie to be as realistic as possible. Even acknowledging how little experience I had in the business, my story fairly jumped off the page, making the other screenplays I'd read in Phil's office look like yesterday's news.

I'm not sure how much I slept that week. I was working all the time. Phil told me twice to take it easy. I couldn't. When the call came from Max Planck's secretary, saying that six Japanese executives would be in town the following week to participate in our meeting, I redoubled my efforts. Phil actually became cross. He said that Ethan was snapping his fingers to make it look as if he was doing something, but we were doing all the work.

The meeting began awkwardly as the group searched for common footing. Ethan introduced each of the men individually, a feat in itself since he wasn't using notes. He then confirmed that the purpose of their visit was to develop a relationship with an American producer who would be willing to work with their corporation in the production of a major feature film. Ethan explained that their corporation primarily manufactured equipment that labeled different kinds of beverage containers. Only five years before, however, the company had introduced a sports drink of its own into the domestic market. "H2 A Go-Go" was an instant and enormous success.

The Japanese men accepted Ethan's description of their corporation with great pride, smiling and nodding to one another and then to us. A few attempts at light banter followed. More accurately, I'd say several tries misfired due to the language barrier.

"But why motion pictures?" Phil interjected. "And why here?"

There was talk about trade cooperation, tax laws, and corporate image-building until Ethan cleared things up. "This company has so much money," he said, "they don't know what to do with it."

The one Japanese man who was most fluent in English spoke briefly about how much they loved American movies.

And then Max Planck took over. Believe me, it's not for nothing that man was such a success. During the next fifteen minutes I felt as if I had crossed the Atlantic with his parents, stood shoulder-to-shoulder with them as they shuffled through immigration on Ellis Island, and then watched as they worked long and tiresome hours in sweatshops so that little Max could have a better life, some hope for the future.

Max introduced us to Keaton and Pickford and Chaplin.

We witnessed the miracle of sound. "Sound," Max said, "as had never been seen before!"

We watched the greatest movies ever made in theaters called the Pantages, the Paramount, and the Chinese, greeted there by men who answered to the names Mayer, Warner, Thalberg, Selznick, and Zukor.

Max told us that an individual named Harry Cohn could not spell the name of the company he ran, Columbia. "A studio," he added, "now owned by a corporation from the same homeland as our guests here today."

Without seeming the least bit self-aggrandizing, Max spoke about the twenty-six movies on which he had been credited as producer or executive producer—and in particular about his two films which had been honored by Oscar nominations. Max hinted that there were several other important movies to which he had contributed in significant ways, including at least one Academy Award-winner, but because of "certain personal commitments" he steadfastly refused to violate, these additional pictures would remain unnamed. Max let us in on some inside information related to the politics involved in nominations to the Academy Awards, intimating that industry veterans were not so concerned with old Oscar as they once had been.

I have sometimes speculated that had our meeting ended there my life might have developed along entirely different lines. I say that because when it came time to review the ideas, which it turned out had been submitted not only under Phil's banner, but by a half dozen other independent producers as well, the one idea that seemed to generate the most heat was none other than mine, synopsized under its working title "Mitch and Me."

It is true that one of the Japanese gentlemen referred persistently to an idea featuring a fictional Japanese baseball player who breaks into the American major leagues. Some gentle persuasion on Max's part, however, was followed by nearly fifteen minutes of intense Japanese-language discussion among the visitors before all present agreed that "Mitch and Me" would be our highest priority. We could make the Japanese-baseball-hero-in-America movie later. If anything, it seemed that the one gentleman's effort to champion the baseball story brought out some latent enthusiasm among the others for "Mitch and Me," and elicited a particular fervor in the individual Ethan identified as being most responsible for the marketing success of "H2 A Go-Go."

There was a brief discussion concerning Hollywood accounting, which Max handled sharply. "Motion picture accounting has become quite standardized," he told Ethan. "I'm not aware of any recent changes made by Sony or Matsushita, if you know what I mean."

Ethan nodded, though for a moment his eyes seemed utterly devoid of reason or confidence. After a long pause he asked, "Do we have a completed screenplay?"

"Oh, don't worry about that," Phil said.

"How can we proceed without a screenplay?" Ethan asked. "Isn't that the first thing you need? How will we know what kind of movie we're going to make?"

"How will we know what kind of movie we're going to make?" Phil replied as if the question were a personal insult. "I'll tell you what kind of movie we're going to make. We're going to make a comedy. That's what we're going to make. A comedy that touches the heart. A film that's broad-based in its appeal, but literate at the same time. A movie that works—and works on multiple levels. What kind of movie are we going to make? A picture people talk about for years. A journey. The journey! An important statement. Unique, too. A classic, that's the word I want. The kind of movie your friends all hate you for. Why? Because it makes so much money and is so damn good at the same time. A good movie, that's what we're going to make. A very good movie. And you're going to be part of it, Ethan." Phil turned toward the Japanese. "You, too."

Phil raised both hands to gesture. "Two thumbs up!" he indicated. "A ten!"

Ethan pressed for more information about the screenplay.

"Sheldon," Phil turned my way and asked, "how does the movie begin?"

"I think we have to establish the setting," I said.

"We have to establish the setting!" Phil repeated in a tone of voice I couldn't read. To be honest, I had the feeling he wanted to kill me. "Small town . . . circus . . . a knock-out opening scene . . . Jesus Christ, Sheldon Green is a fucking genius! A genius! Max, the kid has some kind of instincts, huh?"

"Look," Max said to Ethan finally, "I'm not going to make an issue out of the screenplay and neither should you. What we have in this room right now is the most important part. The idea. A very big idea."

Yeah, I thought. And the money.

For the next half hour we talked about my movie. "Will there be sex?" one of the Japanese men asked.

Another of the visitors responded quickly in Japanese. I heard a word that sounded like "chinpanjii."

Everybody laughed.

I've been told that doing business with Japanese corporations can be an extremely time-consuming process riddled with frustration and wasted effort. What happened to us was nothing of the sort. By the time our meeting broke, Max had secured a firm commitment. The corporation these gentlemen represented would contribute half—and exactly half—of our production costs. Ethan mentioned that paperwork would follow. We closed the meeting with talk about internationalism, the pursuit of world peace, and how it's better not to put too much green horseradish in the soy sauce when eating sushi.

As we were leaving, one of the Japanese men took Max aside. "Excuse me," he said. "Are you a descendant of Max Planck, the Nobel Prize winner?"

Max put his arm over the man's shoulders. "Yes."

Riding the elevator down to the parking garage, Max turned to Phil. "Maybe there's a dance left in the old girl yet," he said.

"I hear music," Phil replied. "I hear music."

"So much for social impact," Phil said during our drive back to the office. He then stated several times that his development efforts were on the verge of being rewarded. Personally, I felt relieved to know that Max

Planck was involved. Max seemed plenty clear about whose idea "Mitch and Me" was, a point I feared might get lost with Phil in a hurry.

My anxiety soared when Phil refused to answer my questions about whether I should begin work on the screenplay.

"You might want to make some notes," he said. "I'd give it a little time though, see if the whole thing doesn't blow over in a day or two."

If nothing else, I'd learned one thing in my screenwriting course. Already I'd rushed a few pages of story line into treatment form and made copies, which I paid for myself outside of office hours, keeping the receipt. At the Writers Guild I paid again, this time to have the pages placed in a sealed and dated envelope in case there should ever be a question as to who created what and when. I assumed, when the attorneys would be called upon years later to break open this envelope in an effort to settle the lawsuit between Phil and me, no one would care about a few typos in the manuscript.

Life In El Lay

With things beginning to percolate in my professional life, I decided to take a more thorough inventory of what was happening in my personal life. Being as dispassionate as possible, it did not take long to complete this task. There was nothing to inventory. Not only were things not going anywhere with Christine, it occurred to me that, other than some misdirected desire on my part, there probably wasn't anything there to begin with. I did see Carrie, the waitress from Seattle, one night at Vince's acting class. I don't know why she made such a big deal of it, but she confirmed that she was going out with one of the guys who'd been with her the night we met at the supermarket.

My situation was so pathetic I felt I could deliver Howard's routine about relationships. "My problem with women," he would say, "can usually be reduced to semantics. I say, 'Yes.' They say, 'No.' But the last time I fell in love, the hang-up was more serious. The girl I was interested in had a bigger penis than I did." Howard would conclude with an imitation of a macho guy who talks as if he's a real lady-killer, but who panics when he calls home and learns that his wife will be back slightly later than usual.

Needless to say, I was discouraged. I thought about how, after four years, I felt so out-of-place in Los Angeles. I considered my lack of personal power, how little money I had, and my urge to run away. I remember feeling as if I was driving the very car that pushed the city beyond the brink—the point at which a paradise could no longer accommodate its inhabitants, the point at which a nice place had turned, without recourse, toward another destiny: 21st-century hell.

I knew there was a group who had beaten me to Los Angeles. These people arrived at a more opportune time, when West Los Angeles, for example, was still open fields. They had gotten theirs and were holding on. Certainly they would not let go easily, not only of the real estate, but of the access, the connections.

This is what I was thinking about when I plowed into the car stopped in front of me. Kimberley says it's inevitable. She says that everyone has an accident in Los Angeles sooner or later. Fortunately no one was hurt. And I was caught up on my insurance payments.

Nursing a glass of iced tea afterwards in a nearby coffee shop, I felt completely out-of-synch. Time seemed to stretch out. When the waitress brought my check, it was hard to focus. The numbers didn't make sense. I couldn't figure the tip.

I walked to a nearby shopping mall to cool off. A security guard told me they were closing and I had to leave. When I finally did settle down, I realized I'd been working too hard. Too much pushing and too much stress.

Howard called me at home the next evening to say that he had given notice at Graphic Toner and started teaching in traffic school. That was convenient. He was able to tell me exactly how many car lengths I should have allowed between my car and the car in front of mine so that I would have had enough room to stop. He was also kind enough to inform me what was going to happen to my insurance rates. Hearing this, I felt as if I had been the one who was rear-ended.

Howard brought me up-to-date regarding his entertainment career. He said that he was appearing at more clubs and, though still not being paid, working more often on nights other than amateur night. He claimed that he was using a considerable amount of new material in his act and suggested I see him perform again soon. With my own cramped living situation (featuring poor relations with Doug), and without much to do at night other than attend Don Blake's screenwriting course or Vince's cold-reading/improvisation class, I was glad to have another choice, someplace to go.

Howard continued to improve as a stand-up. He learned to condense his material into fewer words, leaving the members of his audience with more to imagine, a chance to fill out what only a few months before he would have been cramming down their throats. When something wasn't funny or wasn't working, he didn't dwell on it as long; he was willing to drop it. I don't want to represent Howard as anything more than he was—a guy desperate for attention—but he was making it easier for people to give it to him, putting more of whatever made him such an effective hustler at Graphic Toner to work for himself as an entertainer. Not surprisingly, I could see that Howard was getting more respect from the other comedians who liked to hang out at the club.

It's hard for me to be honest about this period of my life. Maybe it only lasted three or four weeks. But I would be lying if I didn't admit—funny as this might sound—that I actually fell in love with Howard. I'm sure that such a confession would shock him. We never discussed it. I don't think he would have any idea. Among other things, I was afraid he might include me in his act. Howard is a guy who likes to have other people around. Looking back, I can see he wasn't that particular about whom. I was as good as anybody.

During this time, I wanted to be with Howard whenever possible. I think we even met once for lunch. I knew I was falling in love with him because my feelings were so similar to those I experienced when falling in love with a woman: something bordering on dread, something painful.

Perhaps it's surprising that I didn't struggle with these feelings more than I did. I didn't have to. The next thing I remember, Howard was constantly on my nerves. He took me for granted. He always assumed I would show up whenever he asked, particularly for his increasingly irregular, last-minute unscheduled appearances. Several times, not only did he forget to leave my name at the door, but I ended up kicking in more than my share at the end of the evening because not all of his other guests contributed enough to cover the tax and tip.

I did run into Madeline, of Graphic Toner fame, again one night at the club. To my surprise, she gave me her home telephone number and told me to call. I waited one week.

"What are you doing?" she asked me on the phone.

"I'm working for Phil Fried."

"No. What are you doing now?"

"This may sound funny," I said. "I'm trying to decide whether I should do my laundry tonight."

"Why don't you come over here?"

"You have a laundry room?"

"No. You're cute," she said. "Come over."

"Now?"

"Yes."

Madeline did not live far away. Her building, The Royal Gardens, was forgettably brown and surrounded by concrete on four sides. There was no garden, not even the obligatory sickly palm out front. Anyone who has spent five minutes in Los Angeles has seen many of these buildings. Madeline's belonged to the sub-species that doesn't have a courtyard or swimming pool.

I rushed over afraid to be late, but when I walked through the open door, Madeline was just pulling herself together and coming out of the bathroom. She lived in a barely furnished, white-walled one-bedroom apartment. Her most imposing piece of furniture, an oversized bed, was clearly visible from the living room. A broken-down sofa sagged about six feet in front of a television set. A yellow telephone, its tangled cord, and an answering machine rested on a small table beside the sofa.

It seemed as if all the doors in Madeline's apartment were open: the front door, the bathroom door, the bedroom door, even the refrigerator door. I peeked in the fridge. There was a half-full clear container of drinking water, a white plastic bottle with driblets of pink liquid protein on its sides, and an orange box of baking soda.

I asked Madeline if she wanted to go out for a drink or something to eat. She didn't. I sat on the sofa; there wasn't anywhere else I could sit. Madeline sat down next to me. She smelled like bubble gum. I was nervous sitting so close to a woman I had been fantasizing about for a long time. We were alone. Madeline didn't mind that my leg and hers were almost touching. I think she enjoyed the power she held over me.

To get to the point, Madeline gave me a blow job on her sofa while we were watching television. I certainly don't deserve any credit for this. She kept her clothing on the whole time. I hardly touched her, except for a little bit on her breasts.

About forty minutes later, Madeline gave me another blow job, this time she insisted that I stand on her bed. Then she told me that she had to go into Graphic Toner the next morning to pick up her paycheck. I can take a hint. I pulled on my pants and said good-night.

My penis hurt in the car on the way home from being rubbed in a different way than usual. Still, I was surprised that the event had provided so little satisfaction. It's not that I didn't enjoy myself, because I did. And it's not that I expected more, because I didn't. It's just that this was only a single drop of experience. What I needed was more like an ocean.

I called Madeline the next morning at work. She was out. She was out when I called again in the afternoon. When I called her at home that evening, she mentioned that her favorite song was playing on MTV. Another song she liked followed her favorite.

"Can I come over?" I asked finally.

"Not tonight," she said.

Her response wasn't entirely negative, I thought. Maybe there was something I could do for her. I considered calling again, but I couldn't. I was too uptight.

I ran into Harold Stern on the Venice boardwalk one Sunday afternoon. Hal—he was going by the shorter name—told me that while waiting for law school to begin he had gotten involved with a non-profit organization called "Nothing Better." The group packaged and sold an elaborate, but empty box one could give as a present in lieu of something more materialistic; the proceeds went to charity. The bigger the contribution, the bigger the box.

What's in it for him? I caught myself thinking. "Sounds worthwhile," I said.

Our conversation turned to Phil. Hal hadn't spent much time in the office, but he did a pretty good imitation of Phil talking on the telephone. "Let me know," he squawked. "You'll get back to me on that, all right?"

Hal congratulated me on my piece in the *LA Weekly*. We exchanged phone numbers and talked about going to see a movie together. Apparently he held no resentment toward me at all. Not that he should have, but I was his replacement.

Never a model of emotional stability, Phil was acting especially short-tempered with me in the office. In fairness to him, I know that Phil was trying to cut back on his medication. Once I pointed out an obvious error in a letter he was about to send and he told me not to bother him with that kind of thing. He was repeating himself all the time, too, using certain phrases which sound good on occasion, but lose their bounce when repeated too many times. Everything was "cut a deal," or "in and out of negotiations over that." And he was picking on me. He kept calling me "a little Sammy Glick."

"Who's Sammy Glick?" I asked Kimberley when Phil was out of the office.

"Sammy Glick?" Kimberley thought for a moment. "I'm not positive, but I think someone named Sammy Glick worked for Phil a long time ago. If I have it right, he's a big shot at one of the studios now and he won't talk to Phil at all."

Even Max Planck mentioned Sammy Glick when he called the office and I picked up the phone. "Phil tells me you're a real Sammy Glick," he said.

I don't like it when something festers. "I have no idea who Sammy Glick is or what he did to Phil," I said, "but if there's any way I can make it up to him, you know I will."

"You're all right, kid," Max said when he stopped laughing. Then he told me that Sammy Glick was not a real person, but a character in a novel. Although I felt stupid when I heard this, it didn't keep me from imagining all kinds of Sammy Glick-like things I could do to Phil.

There was something else I heard that week I didn't like: the word "package." Phil was talking "package" on the phone with agents and friends. In addition to the star (whom I thought we all agreed we didn't need), directors' names, and, even worse, screenwriters' names were being bandied about.

"Forget what you heard in that meeting," Phil told me when I pressed him. "This thing is not going to develop the way you think it will."

When Phil implied that I was not fulfilling my job responsibilities in relation to the parking lots, I really began to sweat. I thought I better have some representation of my own, meaning an attorney. In a panic, I tried to reach screenwriter Peter Yergin on the studio lot where he'd told me his new deal was going to be. It took me four calls from pay phones to get through; I didn't want to leave a message. Only on my last quarter, when judging by his tone of voice Peter picked up by mistake, did we finally connect. Peter asked me one or two questions before referring me to an attorney named Martin Falklands. Then Peter gave me the brush-off. He told me that he was extremely busy in his new set-up and when things slowed down he would give me a call. Peter's secretary did call me about ten weeks later to apologize for Peter being so busy—about nine weeks after Phil got a call from Peter's agent who'd heard that Phil was developing an idea and looking for a writer.

It's not difficult to understand why I felt so irritated during what should have been the most wonderful period of my life. Phil had me scrunched up at a desk, calling strangers whose names I found in the *Hollywood Creative Directory* about investing in parking lots. Meanwhile he was enjoying slow meetings with writers and directors—mostly people who had cut their teeth on prime time television and commercials—with the door to his office closed. As I remember, the first director candidate dropped by dressed in a football uniform complete with shoulder pads. The second did not wear shoes. The third did not wear deodorant.

When Bobby Savino stopped by, I wanted to thank him for having encouraged me to write. Phil cut me off by practically slamming his office door in my face.

I felt so isolated. Not only did I not know anybody on a personal basis, I didn't know who "anybody" was. And with this recent flurry of activity, when I'd overhear Phil drop this name or that name or talk about so-and-so's comeback or someone else's absolute flop, I had no idea what was going on. Some days while sitting at my desk, I thought I might disappear.

My hell was compounded when a post-production supervisor at one of the studios, someone I had contacted in regard to the parking lots, began to call back after inheriting a good hunk of money. Under ordinary circumstances, his call might have lifted my spirits, made me feel more productive. But I felt worse. Here I was, nothing but a big fake, and somebody was buying my act.

Fortunately, attorney Martin Falklands returned my call almost immediately. Unfortunately, I had foolishly given his secretary our office phone number and Martin called when Phil was around. Not wanting Phil to be aware of what I was doing, I made an excuse and ran down the street to a pay phone in the lobby of another building.

"Mr. Falklands is in conference," his secretary said on the phone. "May we get back?"

"I'm going to be out the rest of the afternoon," I lied. "Would you check again, please?"

"I'm sorry," she said. "Is there another number we could try?"

"No," I said. "I'll try again later."

When I finally did reach Martin Falklands, I told him the whole story about Ethan and the Japanese investors, Max, Phil, and the story called "Mitch and Me."

"Cute idea," Martin interrupted. "I don't have to hear the whole thing now." He then asked if I was afraid I was going to be squeezed out by my boss.

"That's right," I said.

"And you don't want to get lost in the shuffle."

"No, I don't." I was amazed how quickly Martin was able to size things up. We made an appointment for first thing the next morning.

Once in Martin's Century City office with its magnificent view of the Twentieth Century-Fox back-lot and The

Los Angeles Country Club, Martin told me that if I retained his services he would immediately call both Max and Phil, but would definitely not write to Ethan or the Japanese investors, because the last thing we wanted to do was to scare anybody off because of a potential dispute over the rights involved. I considered his proposed phone calls to be a rather severe step. Martin assured me that Max and Phil would both respect the move. Since I was afraid that Phil would fire me after receiving his call, Martin spent five or ten minutes convincing me that Phil would be making a mistake if he did. "This business is not about being polite," he said. "You have to protect yourself. Phil knows that, believe me."

Looking at the mountain of documents, journals, and correspondence piled on his desk I wondered how Martin could possibly remember all the details related to my situation. "I do this kind of thing all the time," he said.

"Do you think I need an agent?"

"Not now."

I wondered, with no one else to look after my interests, if Martin was trying to take advantage of me.

"Do you still represent Peter Yergin?" I asked.

"No."

"Do you think it's strange that Peter's agent called Phil after I told Peter about what was happening in our office?"

"Word gets around," Martin said. "Maybe Peter mentioned it to his agent. Maybe not. In any case, we have other things to worry about now."

Martin informed me that new clients of his firm were required to make an initial payment.

"Why?" I asked.

He looked at his watch.

Martin was right. Phil did not fire me. But I was right, too. As the parade of potential writers, directors, and production managers continued to march past my desk, Phil put me, if possible, into an even deeper freeze. For the better part of two weeks, he chose not to speak to me at all. On those occasions he needed to communicate with me, he would hand a note to Kimberley with instructions that she pass it to me when Phil was out of the office again.

As it turned out, Martin settled things quickly. Apparently, Max Planck always assumed once the appropriate financing was in place that I would write the first screenplay for an absolute minimum fee as if we were making a low budget picture.

As I imagined, Phil was playing games. He admitted to Martin that he had hesitated about letting me write the screenplay—I was a novice. But Phil denied trying to wrest story credit from me.

"Is it fair that I should write a screenplay for an absolute minimum amount?" I asked Martin.

"Do you realize how difficult it is to get a first credit on a feature film?" he responded. "It's so valuable you should almost be willing to do the work for free."

"For free?" I asked. "What kind of attorney are you?"

"Talent," Martin explained patiently, "is usually rewarded 'next time.' Just pray this deal comes to fruition. If they spell your name right in the credits and the audience laughs twice, you'll be well on your way. The best thing that could ever happen to you is for someone else to make a lot of money off your first screenplay. There are writers in this town who have generated entire careers out of one success, getting paid over and over for work of lesser quality—work which often doesn't even make it to the big screen—due to their first break. And maybe the right personality . . ."

I spoke with Martin a number of times over the next few days. He issued a "letter of agreement" between Max Planck and me. A copy went to Phil.

About a week later, Phil called me into his office. "You don't have to sit down," he said. "I just have one thing to tell you."

"What's that?" I asked.

Phil smiled. "You're not going to direct this movie," he said. "Don't even think about it." He picked up his briefcase and left to go home.

The next time I saw Max I asked him if I was foolish to have proceeded without an agent. "When the time comes, I'll introduce you to an agent," he said.

I wondered if he was taking advantage of me, too.

Girl Trouble And Other
Positive Developments

Idecided to have my car's front bumper and grill repaired. Sometime in the future, I would need to pop the hood open. The estimator at the body shop offered to paint the whole car for not much more money. It's amazing what this coat of paint did for my social life. If I didn't know better, I'd say it was the turning point.

Several times while waiting for fast-food or while filling my tank at a self-serve gas station, I sensed that a particular woman was hoping I would speak to her. It seemed as if people were smiling, giving me that special nod of respect I had previously seen bestowed upon others.

One night, cruising alone in my freshly painted car without anything on the agenda, I noticed an opening at an art gallery on La Cienega Boulevard. Why not check it out? I thought.

As I walked into the gallery, a thin blonde who looked as if she might be young enough to attend high school handed me a card on which to record my annual income. Casually, I deposited it into the trash container next to the reception table, a move which apparently established my net worth as being sufficient to attend. However, I mention this event because of one very seductive woman who wore an extremely low-cut dress and who kept eying me throughout the evening. As we circled the room separately, I chose to avoid her, but there was definitely a tension between us.

Even Kimberley was treating me differently. We went out for a drink one night after work, something we had never done before. Sitting in a booth during happy hour with a lot of people squeezing into the place for the free hors d'oeuvres, Kimberley touched me on my thigh and complimented me on the way I was handling Phil. "I like that in a man," she said twice. When her girlfriend arrived, Kimberley invited me to sit with them for a while.

But to really show how well things were going, I ran into a woman named Jill at the laundromat whom I had known in college. She and I had been very close buddies during two of the three years we were in school together. She had even met my parents once when she was passing through Cleveland. To make a long story short, I had a tremendous crush on Jill the entire time I knew her. Unfortunately, she was the girlfriend of a very good friend of mine. I once suspected that Jill and I were on the verge of becoming "a thing" ourselves, but then she and her boyfriend got back together.

Jill surprised me by saying that she had been in Los Angeles for almost three months and was considering the possibility of a permanent move. In the meantime, she had found a convenient sublet. "I like the idea of living in a new place," she said, "although I haven't met many people or found much to do. I'm so bored."

I must admit it was embarrassing to pretend that I didn't notice the panties and bras she was folding as we spoke. But she seemed pretty relaxed about it. Why should I care?

Jill wore an Ace bandage on her right wrist. I asked her about it.

"I hurt myself playing tennis," she said. "It's really painful. I can't write."

"Neither can I," I said and laughed. Then I had to explain that I was working on a screenplay.

"You know what's funny?" she said. "I actually thought about calling your parents to get your phone number."

"You're kidding?"

"I'm not."

Before we said good night, Jill showed me that it was more effective to put detergent into a washing machine beneath the dirty clothes, as opposed to the way I had been doing it: putting the clothing in first and the detergent on top.

Thinking back, I have to wonder why I took so long to call Jill. It's not that I wasn't thinking about her. To the contrary. When I passed the camera store, I realized that my crush on Rhonda was almost gone. And when Madeline called me because her car was in the shop and she needed a ride to an important audition, I asked if there was a number where I could reach her later.

Jill admitted to me on our first date that she had known I was drunk when I finally called. But she said that having decided she wanted to go out with me, she hadn't made a big deal out of it.

After dinner at a Thai restaurant, we couldn't decide on a movie we both wanted to see so we went back to Jill's apartment. She brought out some pictures of friends from college (most of whom I knew) doing crazy things like painting their faces purple and sticking pencils up their nostrils.

At one point, Jill leaned over the photo album in such a way that her blouse fell open slightly. She had a bra on, but there was still a considerable amount of skin showing. Somehow I got the impression she knew exactly what was going on. And so as we were talking, I slid my arm over her shoulder. She didn't object. I let my hand slide down and around so I was touching her breast. Just as I was about to kiss her, she gave me a big smile and put her hand right on my zipper.

Talk about a good sign!

Jill and I began to see each other regularly, meaning we had a standing date on Saturday night, unless one of us was busy in which case we switched it to Friday night. I won't claim my affection for Jill included the fairy tale feeling I had once expected in terms of a boyfriend-girlfriend relationship. I understood why I had been so attracted to her in college—her dirty-brown hair was still thick and playful, dimples appeared when she smiled. But something had changed in me. I was no longer under the same spell. Granted, Jill was fairly together as a person, very good with logistics, and unfailingly enthusiastic about sex. There was also something, I must confess, about sleeping with a girl I had wanted so badly in the past that made me feel as if I was making progress in life.

Jill and I might have had a longer run except for one unfortunate incident. On a lark, we decided to go to a drive-in movie. While we were kissing during the second feature, which we both had seen, I accidently spilled a soft drink onto her lap. Jill was upset and felt I was taking the situation too lightly when I suggested that she take off her dress in the car. Then I had to say that what just happened would make a great scene in a movie. It might not have been so bad when I said this the first time, but I probably should have let it rest. By the time I offered to reimburse her for her dry cleaning expenses, she was quite unhappy. I believe I also made a tactical error during the talk we had when we got back to her apartment. I told Jill that I didn't think she needed to wear so much make-up because she really was a pretty girl.

"I'm dating an infant," she said before asking me to leave.

Jill and I did see each other several times over the next few weeks—more out of habit, I suppose, than anything else. One night, for instance, when we returned to her apartment after dinner I said good night almost immediately. We hadn't eaten much; I had only drunk two beers. But I felt tired. I just wasn't in the mood to sit on her couch and eat ice cream.

As soon as I got home and started to write, I felt wide awake again. Even after Doug interrupted me to discuss the phone bill, I was able to resume working without a hitch. It was almost scary the way that "Mitch and Me" was pouring onto the paper. I suppose it is easier writing dialogue for a main character who can't speak. On the other hand, it can be tricky keeping things believable.

Around two-thirty the very same morning, after an absolutely tremendous writing session, I still had so much energy that I wanted to go out again. Since it was a week-end night, I drove to an all-night dance place.

When I arrived, I felt a wave of guilt wash over me. It struck me that I had never apologized properly to Jill for what happened at the drive-in, and perhaps, in general, I should be treating her with more respect. As late as it was, I marched straight to the pay phone hanging on the wall between the men's and women's bathrooms. A woman was already talking on the phone, seemingly in no hurry to move along. Another woman was waiting for the phone, too. The second woman was stunning.

Rather than get locked into my plan, as I might have in the past, I decided to go for it. And so when this woman turned around, I was prepared. "Name, rank, and serial number," I said.

"What's it to you?" she asked.

My heart was racing a mile a minute. "My name is Sheldon Green. I've just been appointed king of the universe, and I want you to be my number-one lieutenant."

She laughed, thank God!

We talked for a while and I was able to get her phone number. When I got home later, I could not for the life of me find the piece of paper with her number on it. I remembered her name—her first name, anyway. You really are a schmuck, I thought.

Over the next few days I felt very, very low. I was so depressed that I'm not sure I was competent to get along with anybody. The only person I could relate to was my attorney, Martin Falklands. It seemed as if he was on my side. Of course, it didn't take long before I was mad at him as well. When I called to ask him a question, he transferred me to a paralegal who acted as if she had memorized the entire California Civil Code and U.S. Constitution. Unfortunately, she didn't know what she was talking about. For example, when she told me how one joins the Writers Guild she had it all wrong. When I finally got Martin on the phone, I told him that I understood what the word "busy" meant, and I wasn't expecting him to get back to me on every matter *tout de suite*, but in the future I wanted to speak with him and him only. Martin stuttered in response.

I realized that I had learned to project some intensity into a situation myself. Perhaps I was coming into my own. I could be an asshole, too.

Phil called me into his office the next morning. "You have a right to know," he said. "It's not all positive. Max Planck has lined up the rest of the financing, but there are certain conditions. Max did it the only way he could. He didn't have a screenplay to work with and he didn't want to risk the wait. For you, it doesn't matter. For Max and for me, we can't afford to be associated—I may as well say it—with a ship that's going down. Max raised the rest of the money from a man named Jack Vella. Does that name mean anything to you?"

I shook my head no.

"Jack Vella runs a video marketing and distribution company. He's a low-budget personality, a salesman who wants to be something more."

"I don't understand," I said. "You're not going to be involved?"

"I've already been involved," Phil said. "Jack Vella wanted control and he was the best Max could do. Maybe Max isn't the superman he used to be. He's getting older—we're all getting older. Maybe Max has slipped a few notches, I don't know. Jack Vella uses a line producer named Cullen McCarthy. The director has yet to be named."

"That doesn't seem right," I said. "If it weren't for you, this whole thing would have never happened."

"Don't worry about me. I've been taken care of. You certainly don't have to worry about Max."

"Wait," I said. "It doesn't make sense. You and Max..."

Phil interrupted. "What's happening with the screen-play?"

"It's going well," I muttered. "I'm almost done."

"How many pages?"

"About ninety-five," I said, "depending how I adjust the margins."

"Once every three or four years something like this happens. Jack Vella doesn't have time to read. Cullen McCarthy doesn't like to read. The Japanese investors don't know how to read English. Do you understand what I'm saying?"

"Maybe."

"Put it in the right format. Keep it in English. If you have any trouble, take a screenwriting class."

"I've already done that."

"Good. They'll still probably replace you at some point, bring somebody in who knows what they're doing. A writer with credits. If you know that ahead of time, you won't be so upset when it happens."

"Phil," I said, mustering every ounce of sincerity I had, "next Monday I'm going to deliver the best screenplay anybody anywhere . . ." Fearful of his reaction, I hesitated.

"Yes?" Phil demanded impatiently.

"The best screenplay anybody's written since *Splash*."

Mitch

Over the next few weeks I was allowed to operate out of Phil's office as I pleased. During this time Doug referred to me as Tarzan with the King Kong script, Max Planck left for an extended vacation in the South Pacific, and Phil didn't say much—I think he was depressed. Although Phil and I did not have a farewell lunch or mark the end of my employment in his office by any other formal means, he did graciously invite me to his family's upcoming Passover dinner.

When Cullen McCarthy (the line producer responsible for seeing that "Mitch and Me" would be completed in a timely manner and under budget) called to say that at least some of our office space had been secured, I said good-bye to Kimberley and left a note for Phil: *Thanks for everything*.

Driving to the studio, I made a slight detour so I could pass the building where I had once worked at Graphic Toner. A temporary construction fence surrounded the property; it looked as if the building was going to be torn down.

A fence surrounded the studio as well. Almost twenty minutes passed before the security guard received clearance for me to enter. Then, because the first parking area was full, another security guard directed me to an auxiliary lot. After that, it took me another fifteen minutes before I was able to find the bungalow with the handwritten sign *Mitch and Me* taped on the door.

I recognized Cullen McCarthy's big voice over the hum of the air conditioners. Cullen was now being paid to do efficiently what Phil was being paid not to do at all. Cullen asked me if I would be around later to talk. I told him that I would be.

Like Phil, Cullen worked with an attractive office manager—a young woman named Kit who had just returned from the Price Club with a BMW full of toilet paper, styrofoam cups, and non-dairy creamer. Kit and I didn't hit it off very well at first. I don't think she liked the way I kept staring at her legs while she was putting the supplies away. Actually, her immediate impression was that I was a studio messenger boy. Even when I introduced myself, it didn't help. Apparently she and Cullen had a problem with the screenwriter on their last picture.

But what seemed to annoy Kit most was that since all our office space was not yet available, Cullen asked her to set me up in his office for the time being. That meant it would be more difficult for her to have Cullen's undivided attention. "Can't you work at home for a few days?" she asked me before Cullen intervened.

Cullen was a much more relaxed person than I had expected. When later that afternoon he asked me to turn my chair around and we officially convened our first meeting, he handed me a couple of screenplays from successful pictures he'd been associated with to give me a feeling for "what works."

"I prefer never to get artistically involved with a screenplay myself," he said. "I'm a hired hand. My job is to see that things get done. As long as you do what you're supposed to do, the only person around here who's going to give you instructions is the director. And as soon as he arrives, we can start the dance."

"Any idea when that might be?" I asked.

"As soon as humanly possible. We've got a casting session scheduled for the end of next week."

Cullen was surprisingly open about his personal life. When I was sitting in the room, he would talk to his wife on the phone about very intimate things. Not only did he not seem to mind my being there, sometimes he would even ask me for advice.

Cullen had met his wife several years before when they were both working on the same picture. She was the production manager; he was the production coordinator. Now she was home with their six month-old son and feeling out of the loop. She insisted—as I was to hear several times while she was waiting for Cullen to get off another line—that just as Cullen was involved in raising their son, she should participate in the production decisions he was making.

I had a strong sense that something sexual had gone on between Kit and Cullen in the past. I also had a feeling that whatever had happened before would probably happen again.

Cullen passed several invitations my way, mostly to industry screenings he couldn't attend. He once intimated that Kit might like to go. When I asked her about the possibility, she flew into Cullen's office, slamming the door behind her. "What are you trying to tell me?" she yelled. "Why do you treat me this way?"

Jack Vella walked into the bungalow while Kit was screaming. If entering at such a moment flustered Jack, he didn't show it. If having Jack there while Kit was bouncing off the walls flustered Cullen, he didn't show it either.

Jack Vella had driven over from his office in Century City to announce personally that noted director Mel Michaels had agreed to terms and would begin work on "Mitch and Me" the following Monday. Jack delivered the news as if, after investing long in corn futures, he had just learned that locusts had destroyed the entire North American crop.

Cullen informed me that Jack Vella had made a career buying and selling the rights to, and then marketing and distributing, videos of B-movies such as Phil used to make. I suspected that Phil's intense dislike for this man was related to Jack Vella's intimate familiarity with Phil's movies, and his knowledge, to the penny, of what they were now worth.

Before I knew what was happening, Jack had his hand clamped on the back of my neck. "More jokes," he said, "more jokes. Sight gags, slapstick, banana peels, men in dresses. Whatever it takes. Laughs, that's what we need. Laughs, laughs, laughs."

I nodded as best I could.

Jack released his grip and turned to Cullen. "We've got our director. The screenplay is shaping up. What we need is the right chimp."

"Is the completion bond company still insisting on two?" Cullen asked.

"You explain it to me," Jack said. "Why do we need another chimp on the payroll?"

After Jack left, Cullen asked me if I was busy.

"No," I said. "Why?"

"Because starting next week we're not going to have much free time around here."

Cullen and I spent the rest of the afternoon drinking tequila shooters in a bar and then playing one-on-one basketball on the driveway in front of his house. The hoop

was set at eight and a half feet so Cullen could dunk at
will.

Within a week of my move to the production office,
Phil began to call me every day. Even knowing that Cullen
was in the same room with me, Phil would demand that I
report to him on how things were going. Sometimes when
Cullen was out, I'd ask Phil for advice on how I should be
conducting myself. "Keep your eyes open and your
mouth shut," was all he would say.

Director Mel Michaels made his appearance late
Tuesday afternoon. He was a thin man with a nervous,
high-pitched laugh. I incorrectly assumed that he would
want to meet with me immediately in order to discuss the
screenplay. He had other priorities. For example, it took
some time before the furniture in his office was arranged
just right.

Kit gave me the inside scoop. "He's never worked with
chimps before," she said. "Only children and porpoises."

I don't know what the correct way is to ingratiate oneself with an ape, but watching Mel work the chimp casting session, I could sense trouble coming. Kit had the
room set up with a big bowl of fruit on a coffee table
backed by chairs for Mel, Cullen, and the casting director.
Newspapers were spread on the floor to one side. Mel
mugged with the chimps, asked them their names, and
when they wouldn't cooperate tried to lead them around
the room by hand. When these gestures proved ineffective
with the chimps, he tried the same tactics with their wranglers.

The casting director, an attractive woman who was
perhaps in her late thirties, suggested that we look at an

orangutan to see if we wanted to explore another direction.

Mel shook my script in her face. "The part is written for a chimp!"

The casting director slumped in her chair and proceeded to glower at each candidate then called to audition. At one point, a chimp made a move for the bowl of fruit. "No," she said, "those are for the producer and director."

Cullen, who could be a pretty spontaneous guy, took the bowl of fruit to the chimp and then as a joke he threw a banana to Mel.

We were running at least a half hour behind when Jack Vella dropped in for a look. One of the chimps waiting in the outer office area for his audition to begin took an immediate liking to our producer. This led to talk that Jack was a natural with apes as well as with people.

"We need to speak," Jack said to Cullen, having seen enough.

"Jokes," he said as he passed me on his way out. "Bad accents, snoring, animals driving. You know what to do."

I nodded.

When Jack left, there was a discussion about how we should proceed. Mel decided that we had made too many concessions to the chimps and that the auditions should be conducted in a more traditional manner. While Kit was copying pages to use from the script, Mel took me aside to discuss the screenplay. "I don't want to embarrass you," he said. "I know it's your first outing, but it still needs a tremendous amount of work."

"Whatever it takes," I replied. "I'll do it."

"Well, don't change anything yet," he said. "Not until we've had a chance to talk."

"I won't."

When it was time to resume our auditions, the first scene we used was set in the family's dining room. The two children—Jenny and Jimmy—are eating with Mitch, who doesn't have much of an appetite. Jenny goes into the kitchen to get Mitch something to eat and brings out boxes of every banana-flavored food imaginable: banana JELL-O, banana pudding, banana cake mix. But Mitch isn't satisfied until he gets a real banana.

Kit played Jenny. Cullen's nephew Jay, who had signed on the day before as a production intern, played Jimmy.

If the hopeful chimp was able to pass this first test satisfactorily, Mel continued with another scene in which Kit stood in to play the cheerleader Mitch takes to the senior prom. Her line *Do you know what I was thinking, Mitch?* becomes the cue for Mitch to throw his arm over her shoulder and gently rest his head on her chest. The cheerleader then turns to the camera and says, "You're not like the other guys, Mitch. You're special." Except for a few screams when one of the chimps got out of line and tried to pull Kit's blouse off, I thought that Kit was remarkably at ease with her assignment.

We must have had ten or twelve chimps pass through the office that morning. However, there was just no question in anybody's mind that one stood out. He projected an aura of success, a winning vibe. He made everybody feel at home, handled himself like a professional, and acted as if he really wanted the job. Equally important, he communicated an attitude that said *team* and God knows we needed that. I mean there were plenty of people running around who acted as if they believed in cooperation, but I'm not sure they really did.

I overheard Cullen speaking to Jack Vella over the phone. "Forget what you saw this morning," Cullen said. "We've got a monkey in here who can deliver the goods." After responding to a series of questions, Cullen told Jack that he would speak to the people in "business affairs" first thing the next morning.

At this point, we took another break—we'd been at it for more than four hours. "Where is Cullen's tuna fish sandwich?" Kit demanded in a voice that echoed throughout the bungalow.

"I'd say it's right between her legs," the production designer whispered to the art director when he thought no one else was listening. I made a mental note to stay on their good side, which I knew would not be difficult since I was both young and male.

Everyone was tired so there was widespread sentiment to cancel the rest of the session. But Cullen reminded us that we had no guarantee that our first chimp would come to terms and furthermore, due to the requirements laid down by the completion bond company, we needed to carry a back-up chimp. When our leading candidate's wrangler saw the list of chimps scheduled to come in later that afternoon, he clued us in about a couple other chimps he thought deserved consideration.

The casting director was defensive. However, we did find our back-up, a chimp who would soon be called Mitch Two, based on a recommendation made by the man who trained Mitch One.

Anxieties that had arisen regarding Mel Michaels, due to the manner in which he conducted the casting session, were eased somewhat the next day when he asked Kit to distribute invitations to selected members of the office for a party the following Sunday at his home in Malibu. I got one.

Kit appeared distraught when I asked her if she was going. She looked as if she had been crying, but she wouldn't tell me why. Later I learned that Cullen was keeping his options open in terms of whom he wanted to accompany to the party, and one of those options was his wife.

Kimberley forwarded a postcard to me from Max Planck. Max's handwriting was barely legible. *Having a wonderful time,* he wrote. *Good luck on the ranch.*

I received my first phone call from an agent. He asked me what else I had going. "This is it," I said. "I want this to be the best picture possible." I noticed there was traffic noise in the background. Car phone, I thought.

"Terrific," he said. "But don't rest on your laurels. Start working on something else now."

"Thanks," I said. "By the way, what made you call?"

"Your movie," he said. "The buzz is good."

Gearing Up

Mel's party was a strange affair. Most people wore black. This created a nice contrast with the house, which and in which almost everything was white. The caterers dressed in black and white. The hors d'oeuvres were delicious—mostly browns, greens, reds, and yellows. The lawn was green, the ocean was blue, and the retriever kept in the side service yard was golden.

Although no one said anything in particular that made me think about this, one thought kept running through my mind, something a friend from a wealthy family once told me. He said that sometimes one sees ducks on a pond and thinks that everything is going smoothly. But one never knows how hard those ducks are paddling beneath the surface.

With a crowd like this, I expected a lot of flirting and talk about sex. I was surprised that most of the conversation seemed to focus on real estate and favorite new restaurants. Among all the different topics, I don't think sex was higher than sixth on the list. It seemed as if people were actually trying not to flirt.

Kit was quite protective of me. Several times she clued me in about what was being said, helped me to read between the lines. Kit and I had decided to drive to

Malibu together because I didn't want to invite Jill, and
Cullen wanted to invite his wife. It's not that I wasn't
interested in seeing Jill anymore; I just didn't want to
involve her so intimately in my world. And I could tell
that Kit didn't want to go alone.

"How are you getting to the party?" she asked me.

"My car," I said. "I guess."

"Why don't we go in mine?" She gave me her address
in Beverly Hills.

"Beverly Hills?" I asked. "You live in Beverly Hills?"

"I was married before," she said.

"Before what?"

"Before now."

Kit had a lot to drink at Mel's. I had more than I'm
used to. There were a number of toasts to the movie, toasts
to a picture that made a positive statement. "And that's
going to make a shitload of money," someone standing
next to Jack Vella said to scattered laughter and applause.

Ethan was in attendance, smiling widely and shaking
lots of hands. "Here's the genius," he said to me at one
point.

At first I wondered if I was imagining things, but after
a while there could just be no question that Kit kept
brushing her breasts against my arm whenever we were
walking together. I was surprised that she would stay so
close to me in the first place and somewhat embarrassed
she would do this in front of so many people. Nobody
paid any attention.

When I took Kit home after the party she invited me in
for a drink.

"Don't you think we've had enough to drink already?"
I replied.

Kit pulled her skirt up an inch or two and let her right
leg flop against the car door. "What are you thinking
about, Sheldon?"

"Nothing," I said.

"Nothing?"

"I mean I was thinking about what a nice party it was."

"That's all?"

"Yes."

She pulled her skirt up some more. "How do you feel right now, Sheldon?"

"Fine."

"What do you feel right now?"

"Fine," I said. "I feel fine."

"You feel fine?"

"Yes, I feel fine."

"Good," she said. "Go home."

Getting out of her car, Kit caught a heel, stumbled, and fell down. Although she stood up quickly as if nothing had happened, we both noticed a trickle of blood running through her panty hose and down her leg. She started to cry.

I helped her to the door. "This house stinks," she sobbed. "I hate Cullen."

Driving home, I felt terrible. I decided to give it some rest, but fully intended to apologize to Kit first thing Monday morning.

Unfortunately, I didn't have a chance. Our bungalow was in an uproar. Everyone's attention was diverted by a crisis created when Cullen foolishly placed himself in the position of having to retract an offer he made for the acting services of Missy Killebrew, star of the hit TV sitcom "Missy" and an obvious candidate for the role of Mom. Mel, instead of being thrilled as Cullen had expected, declared Missy to be an absolutely wrong choice for the part. (Later I learned that Missy was a distant cousin of Mel's first wife.) Cullen tried to cover his tracks with promises of a better role for Missy in his next project, "a bigger picture." Missy's agent wasn't buying it. He wanted full payment for his client—at a minimum—whether she performed or not. Two attorneys from business affairs established a command post in the bungalow's kitchenette.

Despite all the confusion, Mel and I held our second meeting regarding the screenplay while we were both waiting to use the bathroom. I'd noticed Mel had a habit of responding to a person's preferences with a contrary opinion. If there was a scene I liked and wanted left intact, the best way to insure that it remained uncut was to tell Mel that I was worried about it.

"Don't be," he'd say. "I can make it work."

Phil stopped by one morning during pre-production. Although Kimberley did call to let me know he was coming, it still felt like an intrusion. Phil marched to my desk in Cullen's office—Cullen was out—and started massaging my shoulders from behind. "Is this the Department of Social Impact?" he asked.

Intuitively, I knew that spending time with Phil Fried was not the best politics. But with production schedules coming together, location permits and agreements being readied, and—the glitch with Missy Killebrew notwithstanding—casting proceeding apace, I figured it wouldn't kill me to spend a few minutes with the man who had given me my start in the business.

Phil suggested the studio commissary.

"Fine," I said.

Standing in line, Phil said that he would pay for lunch, insisting there be no discussion.

"That's not necessary," I said.

"All right, we'll go dutch."

For the most part, Phil and I ate together in silence. It seemed as if we had nothing to say. Toward the end of our meal, however, Phil reminded me that Saturday was the first night of Passover. He had me write down his brother Sandy's home address and practically demanded that I attend.

"Thanks," I said. "I'll be there."

Sandy greeted me warmly. He was serious-looking, shorter and more solidly-built than his brother. Although I had worked in Phil's office for a long time, I had never actually met Sandy in person. But he seemed fully informed as to who I was. He immediately invited me to take a tour of the house, making sure that I understood at what stage in his family's history each room had been built or remodeled. He took particular pleasure along the way in pointing out a number of photographs that featured himself and other somber-looking men standing in front of parking lots, kiosks, and ramps. The oldest pictures were taken in New York.

I met Mrs. Sandy Fried as our tour concluded in the kitchen. She was surrounded by children and grandchildren. One granddaughter, a college freshman, told me her goal was to work in the motion picture business.

"*Oy,*" Mrs. Fried said, when she heard her granddaughter telling me what she wanted to do with the rest of her life, "like Uncle Phil."

Altogether I'd say there were more than thirty people seated around the three tables set up in the living room. To my embarrassment, and almost before I knew what was happening, everyone was asking me about the movie. I tried to play this down, but it was hard to avoid. Everybody was so knowledgeable about the business. There was another outbreak of questioning about the movie as the gefilte fish was being served and again while the children were searching for the hidden matzo.

Phil arrived in time for the third cup of wine. He said his three-year old daughter was not feeling well and his wife was under the weather, too. He claimed both were sorry about missing dinner and sent their love to everyone. After spending so much time with the man, I knew he was lying. I wasn't sure what the Frieds' real ailment was, but I knew it wasn't the flu.

Sandy concluded the service with lots of disapproving looks to the two empty folding chairs where Phil's wife and daughter were supposed to sit. Although Sandy called on us individually to read from the *Haggadah*, he saved the most dramatic passages for one grandson who was able to read the Hebrew text as well as its English translation. When the boy stumbled with a word, Sandy was quick to help. Finally, the flustered grandson turned to Sandy and said, "Why don't you read it?"

I arrived home carrying a doggy-bag full of coconut macaroons and matzo. Entering, our apartment looked worse than usual. "Doug?" I called out.

No reply.

Coming home once before, I had the feeling that things weren't right. On that occasion, Doug had removed the framed copy of the *LA Weekly* featuring my article on the intersections which I'd hung above the sofa bed. I found it later in the closet.

This time Doug's TV and VCR were gone. We'd been robbed.

The drawers in my dresser were upended on the floor; my clothes were scattered around the room. I put everything in order as best I could. Then I checked the hallway, the lobby, and the parking area—anywhere I might find a clue as to what happened. Everything appeared as usual. I walked to the alley behind the building. There was nothing to see.

I called the police. The first time I dialed, the number was busy. The second time I got a recording. The third time I was put on hold before being disconnected.

I felt incredibly anxious. I needed to speak to someone. I called Jill. She wasn't home. Impulsively, I dialed Carrie.

"Is it too late to go out for a drink tonight?" the words blurted out of my mouth.

"There's no way," she said. "Even if I wanted to see you, my dog just threw up."

Her rejection barely registered. With production about to begin, I could almost forget about how much I hated my life in Los Angeles.

Almost, but not quite.

Happy

The next morning, I woke in a complete panic. For a moment, I didn't know what time it was, where I was supposed to be, or if there was a bill that needed to be paid. Sitting up, my panic lifted slightly. I realized I was going to have to step on it or I would be late for the first day of production.

Stumbling into my pants, however, my head cleared. I thought: if last night was Saturday night, this must be Sunday morning. Feeling somewhat relieved, I had a good laugh at myself. Then I went back to sleep.

Monday morning, when I did arrive on location in the San Fernando Valley, most members of the crew were standing around drinking coffee. A couple of beefy-looking guys carried lighting equipment and electrical gear into a modest-sized middle-class house, the first set we would use for "Mitch and Me." Cullen kept a cellular phone close to his ear; he certainly looked to be in his element. To the extent he was responsible, I felt the overall tone was just right.

In a very minor glitch, both chimps arrived with their managers when only Mitch One was expected on-site. Mitch Two was to be "on call," off-site, at half the daily rate. He was to receive his full salary only when his presence was actually required. After a brief discussion, Cullen and the production manager agreed that the second chimp would be paid full salary for that day's work only. The chimp's handler agreed in the future to comply with the original plan as Cullen had understood it from the beginning.

Mitch One shared a camper with his wrangler who rented the trailer to the production company at an exorbitant rate. The second chimp and his handler had their own camper as well. A friendly, if slightly tense moment occurred when the two chimps were checking out each other's accommodations. Mitch Two had a special swing set. Mitch One didn't. When Mitch One tried to sit in the swing, Mitch Two became territorial. Mitch One's wrangler resolved the situation by offering Mitch Two a couple boxes of Raisinets.

On the set, Mitch One turned out to be even more of a ham than we had hoped. He liked to mug for the crew and had a knack for picking pockets of handkerchiefs, combs, and wallets. He was such a player that within an hour after we started filming, Cullen had to ask the production manager to clear the set of anyone not directly involved in the scene being shot in order not to distract the little ape. This restriction included me. I found myself standing next to the snack table loaded with fruit, peanut butter, juice, candy, and donuts. The donuts reminded me that I should be thinking about another screenplay.

As I was finishing my third donut, I began to speak with a young woman who introduced herself as our "craft service" person. Craft service, she told me, is responsible for setting up the snack table and for keeping the location site clean and in reasonable order. This means running around with a broom and trash bag and cleaning up whatever messes there are. I wish I had asked for her phone number right away because it turns out that she felt she'd spent too much time in the business to work on a picture whose messes included those of two chimps.

Everyone thought we were off to a good start. But a problem with one of the camera lenses discovered late in the morning meant that we would have to do some reshooting.

Lunch was delicious. I promised myself several times I wouldn't eat so many donuts again. The catering company really laid it out the first day. There were barbecued steaks, a curried red snapper dish, pasta with smoked chicken, and lots of sautéed vegetables, salads, and fresh fruit. Although the chocolate cake was lousy and reminded me of the stuff served in my elementary school cafeteria, overall there really wasn't much to complain about.

Jack Vella made his appearance during the lunch hour, crushing my hand en route to speak with Cullen. Mel didn't eat anything. I overheard him mumbling to the director of photography about having involved himself with another "porpoise" movie. On the other hand, Cullen was definitely up. And when Kit arrived in her BMW with paperwork for Cullen to sign, she radiated nothing but confidence and well-being. How quickly things change, I thought, remembering what a mess she was after Mel's party.

Toward the end of lunch, some members of the cast and crew stepped forward with cupcakes the caterer had specially prepared and we all sang "Happy Birthday" to Mark Jason Lyle, who would be introduced to the movie-going public in the role of youngest family member Jimmy. Markie was celebrating his eighth birthday.

"How does it feel to be eight?" I asked.

"Better," he said.

By late afternoon our situation had become more critical. We had yet to complete the first shot of the day. Cullen was constantly on his cellular phone. It looked as if he was doing a lot of explaining. We hadn't anticipated any problems with the first scene: Mom (played by Bonnie Hayden, best known for her work on the hit series "Get Me Out of Here!") collapses exhausted on a couch in the living room, having just returned from her part-time job at McDonald's. She calls to the other room: "Mitch, get me a Coke, would you?"

The second shot, which we also failed to get, shows Mitch going into the kitchen; seconds later, he emerges with a Coke. The third shot shows Mitch handing the Coke to Mom, which she takes without turning around.

By this point, the only people allowed in the house were Mel, the director of photography, each of their first assistants, two people responsible for lighting, the script supervisor, our set dresser, a couple of hair and make-up people, one person from wardrobe, Bonnie, Mitch One, his wrangler, and a woman from the Humane Society who claimed she was visiting the set to make sure the chimps were being treated properly. (I don't know if we scared her off or if everything appeared to be all right; this was the only day I saw her.)

Forty other people, including one very nervous homeowner, stood in front of the house waiting for any sign of progress. I remember being under constant admonition from the second assistant director to "Please, please, please keep it down, people."

It was frustrating to stand outside. I wanted to help, to do something to contribute.

"Everything is under control," the production manager told me in response to my suggestion that I observe the proceedings from a stool placed behind the camera. "You'll just be in the way."

Occasionally some applause emanated from the house. At first we assumed this meant a scene had been successfully taken. But as the afternoon wore on, the applause began to indicate only that a rehearsal had gone well. Later the applause became a sign that someone had been able to get Mitch out of the director's chair. I remember a discussion on the front lawn involving Mel, Cullen, and the director of photography—a discussion everyone else was straining to hear. A decision was made to allow the camera to roll continuously in an effort to capture Mitch at his more spontaneous self, as we had seen him in the bungalow when he wasn't dealing with words he didn't understand such as "Rolling," "Speed," "Action," and "Goddamn it!" Several times I saw Cullen looking my way; I had a good notion of what was on his mind. He was trying to decide whether I could further simplify the scenes. However, the three shots included only one line: *Mitch, get me a Coke, would you?*

Around six-thirty, there were some words on the front porch between Mel and Mitch One's handler. At six forty-five, Mitch Two, who had been allowed to visit the set only during the lunch break, was shuttled into the house for a try himself. Finally, around seven, when there was no way we could continue without the crew going into "golden time" at twice their normal pay, Cullen and Mel burst out of the house and began an all-too-public discussion, capped when Mel yelled, "Just get me some monkeys who can act!"

"I'll take care of it," Cullen said.

Mel stomped back into the house. Cullen sighed and followed.

The production manager emerged shortly thereafter with instructions that we would assemble again in the morning an hour earlier than previously scheduled.

Day Two did not go much better. Although everything was in place, Mel could not make it work. By the end of Day Two, Mel looked as if he was standing at the edge of a cliff, eyes fixed on unforgiving rocks below.

Twenty minutes after we wrapped Day Two, I watched an overheated Mel screaming at Cullen in the parking area. "Burritos are popular, too," he yelled. "Why don't we make a movie about burritos?"

I didn't want to say anything so I got into my car. But I had seen an announcement in *Variety* about a movie titled "Burrito Afternoon."

At six the next morning, Mitch One and Mitch Two were both on the set. There was a psychologist on board who specialized in working with animals. And we had a new director. His name was Prescott Lansing.

"Prescott is exactly what this movie needs," Cullen told me.

"What's that?"

"Someone who knows how to handle talent."

Apparently Prescott grew up near the San Diego Zoo. Over the years, he had successfully completed a number of major projects with animals, including the choreography for a wild animals circus act in Las Vegas. Prescott managed to parlay his early success into a career directing television commercials. His multi-award-winning signature piece was a car commercial which featured an elephant, and also happened, as fate would have it, to include a chimpanzee. As if all this wasn't enough to qualify him as the man for the job, Prescott was widely recognized as the force behind *Caramba!*, the story of a frightened, wild tiger that terrorizes a co-ed jungle expedition. *Caramba!*, which was shot in Vancouver, British Columbia, grossed twenty-eight million dollars and cost less than four.

The first thing Prescott did, in full view of cast and crew, was to read my screenplay.

He laughed a couple times.

Which page? I wondered.

"All right," Prescott said when he finished reading fifteen minutes later. "Let the games begin."

Prescott certainly proved to be more effective than Mel. I think he had a special way with chimps.

One scene that worked especially well and which gave everyone an added measure of confidence in Prescott's ability to get the job done involved the youngest child, Jimmy (played by Markie Lyle). Mitch and Jimmy are enjoying a game of chess in the living room. Dad comes in from the kitchen, sees only the chessboard, and says, "Mitch, you've got to protect your king!" I knew chimpanzees have a natural propensity to scratch their heads; I thought the scene would play easily. Still, I had no idea what a professional director could contribute. Prescott transformed a simple scene into a virtual laugh riot.

Prescott was less sensitive with people than he was with chimpanzees. When he asked someone a question, he would immediately take on a pained, disapproving expression before he even heard the answer. As the person he was questioning responded, Prescott would frequently say, "Yeah," but in the most dismissive way. He rarely gave a clue as to what he was thinking himself.

At lunchtime, Prescott allowed about five people, including the director of photography, the first assistant cameraman, and me, to stand ahead of him in line. My initial reaction was that he was using us to see which items looked most appetizing and to make sure he would not be poisoned. But Prescott had a way of flattering people, too. "Did you really write this?" he asked me.

Being modest, I allowed the first assistant cameraman to say, "You did, right?"

I nodded.

The director of photography added, "It's your first screenplay, isn't it?"

I nodded again.

"That's fantastic," Prescott said. "It's hard to believe."

Prescott opened up to me about his own life as we were carrying our paper plates and utensils to the trash cans. "I'm the only person in Hollywood who can do 'flake,'" he said, "and still eat three meals a day."

"Flake?" I asked loudly.

"Ssshhhh!" Annoyed, he looked over his shoulder to make sure that no one had heard me. "Cocaine," he mouthed the word.

The rest of the crew were easier to figure out. The creative people often acted as if they were revisiting that time of life known as "the terrible two's." They were all right if left to themselves and given a very loose outline of what was needed. But put any pressure on them and as soon as their immediate supervisor was out of earshot, they would throw a snit. Those members of the company working what might be described as the blue collar jobs spent most of their time discussing home buying, mort-

gages, previous jobs, union dues, and whatever was left in
their garages that could still be rented to the production.

A much greater surprise than Mel's replacement
occurred at the start of the second week, when an uniden-
tified team of studio executives paid an unscheduled visit
to our location. Coupled with Cullen's absence, the event
fueled rumors about the future of our production. I
remember a lot of dire speculation and nervousness on
the set. One rumor circulating was that Jack Vella's company had run into serious cash-flow problems, and we
would each be forced to contribute one-thousand dollars
of our own money so that production could continue.

By afternoon, the truth was out. Jack Vella had sold all
his rights to the major studio with whom he had previously inked the domestic distribution agreement. Some
younger members of the crew were anxious about what
this would mean regarding their employment. Old-
timers, however, interpreted the news as assurance that
paychecks would clear.

Studio executives, I'm told, are paid the "big bucks" to
make correct decisions regarding complex creative problems and to do so quickly. I can only marvel at what the
group that visited our set determined. Because—as evi-
denced by the Missy Killebrew fiasco and the need to
replace Mel Michaels—these executives decided that
Cullen McCarthy had lost control. They also determined
that Max Planck and Philip Fried had been prematurely
ejected from the production. By their lights, the best
remedy was to get Max and Phil involved again immediately, if they would agree to terms.

When I rushed back to the bungalow, I was so amazed to see Phil standing there that I wanted to know every detail. He didn't have time. "Suffice it to say, I'm back."

He then proceeded to throw me out of what had been Cullen's and my office, but would now be his. Logistically, this wasn't difficult since whoever had moved Cullen's things managed to remove most of mine at the same time.

Although it never feels good to be evicted, Phil did go to some lengths to see that I was set up with a decent office of my own. I soon had two private phone lines, a nice sofa, and plenty of room and privacy to work comfortably or take a nap.

I didn't know why Kit couldn't stay on when Cullen left, but I was quite happy to see Kimberley again. She and I had a conference of our own in front of the bungalow where workmen were already repainting the pavement so that Max and Phil could have the two most prominent parking spaces.

"Where's Max going to sit?" I asked. "The bungalow is pretty crowded."

"You're kidding, right?" Kimberley paused, waiting for me to admit that I was.

"Don't look at me that way," I said. "How am I supposed to know?"

"Planck's office will be over there," she said, pointing at the two-story building next door.

The following morning Phil appeared on location dressed in a khaki safari outfit featuring short pants, but which still qualified technically as a one-piece jumpsuit. He wore a whistle around his neck and carried a clipboard. Max Planck, despite having flown continually for the past twenty-four hours, made his appearance dressed in an elegant charcoal gray suit, a blue silk shirt, and the reddest tie I have ever seen. Max didn't spend much time with me, either. But I knew he was being businesslike, not curt, and that others had more of the answers he needed.

Phil's first challenge was to ease a tension that had developed between the transportation department and the location manager. The Teamsters had been disregarding the location manager's carefully detailed maps and were parking in the red zone on the wrong side of the street. When a motorcycle policeman arrived, the drivers were hanging around the catering truck eating breakfast burritos and donuts and drinking coffee. The location manager urged the Teamsters to move their trucks so as not to jeopardize the permit he had arranged with the city. The drivers were slow to act.

I thought Phil handled the situation admirably. Mincing no words, he told the captain of the transportation department to have his men move the trucks immediately. And then to show that he was being fair all around, he forcefully told the location manager in front of everyone else that he never wanted to hear about this problem again.

The next afternoon an even more difficult problem arose. Prescott was struggling with a scene featuring not only Mitch, but also Happy, the family dog. Concerned that artistic differences might render a dog and chimp incapable of working together, both Prescott and the production manager asked me several times whether I thought the scene was crucial to the narrative. I conceded it was not. However, I did think it would be a nice touch to show Happy trying to warn the parents that Mitch was not who he seemed to be. And there was a line I hoped we could keep, delivered when Jimmy recognizes that Happy is distraught. "Look, Mom," he says. "Happy is sad."

Prescott, who had nailed every scene to date, tried valiantly to make it work. Several times he demonstrated for both Happy and Mitch—and their respective wranglers—exactly what he wanted. The animal psychologist became involved too, working first with Mitch in his trailer and then with Happy in the back yard. Finally, the psychologist brought both animals together on the driveway in an effort to sort out the problem.

Prescott had a tremendous amount of credibility with all concerned so when he said, "No way," this carried great weight.

Phil had made a point to stay away from the camera and out of Prescott's hair, but when Happy snapped at Mitch, he decided it was time to intervene. Laying his clipboard on a bench, Phil marched into the house.

"Just what are you trying to achieve?" he asked the animal psychologist.

Even before the psychologist could respond, Phil started yelling. "You couldn't make it with people? That's why you're working with animals? Get the fuck off my set! Get off my set now!"

It's probably a good thing I was around. "Phil," I said six or seven times, "he's only trying to help."

"Chimp psychologist," Phil muttered as the poor guy was picking up his toys and box of colored milk bones. "Not on my set."

After a few more failed takes, Phil turned to Happy, the dog. "You're fired, too."

Wild-eyed, Phil looked around the room to see who else he could fire.

"Why don't we call it a wrap?" Prescott instructed the first assistant director.

Everyone scrambled to get off the set as quickly as possible.

The Girlfriend From Hell

Phil was all business. Without hesitation he authorized payment to the owner of the house we were using as compensation for the built-in bookshelves Prescott had ordered removed to make room for a better camera angle.

In contrast to the all-knowing, do-nothing shill I had once helped raise money for parking lot investments, Phil was a blaze of action. He was Sky King, the Lone Ranger, and Captain Kirk all rolled into one.

If anyone did anything Phil didn't like, he summoned the offending party into his office. "I realize you were operating on a certain understanding based on the way things used to be," he said, "but I'm the producer now."

One afternoon Bobby Savino showed up.

"Bobby!" Phil proclaimed, giving him a warm smile and a big hug. "I'll have Kimberley call you. We'll make a lunch date." Then he showed Bobby the door.

Bobby's expression was so pitiful. Don't look at me, I wanted to say. But for the grace of God . . .

Again, on the set I had asked the production manager if I could help. "Frankly," he said, "I prefer not to have the writer around."

I knew that the single most productive thing I could do was to begin work on another screenplay. But the few times I actually sat down to write, I couldn't concentrate. It was so much easier to get into my car and drive to wherever we were shooting.

From my vantage point next to the catering truck, I observed a friendship develop between Markie Lyle and Mitch One. I had written the character Jimmy to be a shy child who feels like he's a fish out of water himself. As the story progresses, Jimmy becomes the first family member to recognize Mitch's true identity. Mitch and Jimmy become co-conspirators; Mitch is Jimmy's first real friend. Off-camera, my fiction became their reality. Markie and Mitch began to hang out together in Mitch One's trailer.

I felt jealous. The few times I approached Mitch One in a casual way, he stiffened noticeably. Mitch One's icy attitude became a joke at my expense. Here I was, the person who had written the movie, and Mitch One wouldn't let me near him without a crowd of other people around.

Perhaps out of loneliness, and with so much time on my hands, I began to call Jill more often. Sometimes, we would go to the movies. Sometimes, we would have something to eat. Almost always, we would go back to her apartment and talk about how important it was to be monogamous. We promised each other several times that if either of us was going to have another sexual partner, that person would inform the other immediately. We also agreed that safe sex massage was the only way to go. Before long, however, we would find ourselves wanting to "do it." But since we hadn't expected to have intercourse, we didn't have any condoms. And so we would end up having sex without a rubber—again.

One night while watching television at Jill's apartment, I felt something furry on my arm. My first reaction was to wonder whether there was a chimp in the house; my second reaction was to sneeze. Jill had adopted a tiny kitten.

"That's nice," I said. "Did you know I'm allergic?" She didn't.

This kitten loved to visit. If we put her in the kitchen, she meowed incessantly and scratched at the door. "Isn't she darling?" Jill asked.

"No."

From that point on, I could only spend about forty-five minutes in her apartment before my eyes would bug out. If I fell asleep after sex, I could usually manage another half hour.

We decided that Jill should come over to my place. Although I felt a certain pride in having a woman over, this satisfaction hardly compensated for our loss of privacy. We did stay at a motel one night. That didn't feel right. I guess we weren't meant to be with each other, after all. I'm not going to blame the kitten.

Since we were shooting scenes of Mitch's high school hijinks, we needed quite a few eighteen, nineteen, and twenty year-old girls who looked as if they were fifteen, sixteen, and seventeen. Having perhaps missed this stage of normal adolescent development myself, these girls were almost exactly my type. The frustrating thing was that the girls seemed more interested in attracting the eighteen-, nineteen-, and twenty-year-old actors who were also working as extras than in getting to know me.

One day during lunch, one of the male extras did the unthinkable. He walked over to Prescott while Prescott was eating and asked him what was good.

The extras coordinator, whose job was to recruit and supervise the extras, flew across the parking lot on which the lunch tables were arranged. She apologized profusely to Prescott and then approached the offending party. "A movie is not a democracy," she lectured the extra. "There is no Bill of Rights. But no one is forced to participate either. So do us all a favor. Go to the catering truck, get yourself some lunch, and don't cause me any more aggravation."

For some reason, the other extras all burst into applause.

The studio's product placement people began to make regular appearances on the set. Following the *Mitch, get me a Coke, would you?* scene, it had become pretty much common knowledge that Mitch One was passionate about the stuff. Prescott made no bones about it. If Mitch One was delivering in front of the camera, he could have all the Coke that he wanted. In one improvised scene, for which I would later be given more credit than I would have liked, Mitch consumes so many cans of Coke that one of his friends goes into a 7-11 and buys him a Super Big Gulp of Coke, which Mitch then practically inhales.

Mitch One's wrangler was concerned because he had never seen a chimpanzee who loved Coke the way that Mitch did. He claimed it wasn't normal. Markie Lyle attempted without success to hide the stuff so that Mitch One wouldn't think about it. I tried to warn Prescott, then Phil. Nobody listened. Nobody cared. People who see the movie will have no idea how much Coke the little chimp really drank because they will see only those scenes which made the final cut.

Mitch Two hated the stuff, a preference which eliminated him from all but the most mundane work. Mitch Two turned his head whenever he was presented with Coke. I'm guessing he would have gone the way of Happy, the dog, if not for the completion bond requirement that we keep two chimps on the picture.

Watching the dailies with Phil and Max in the office one morning, the movie looked like a complete mess. Even allowing for the fact we were shooting scenes out of sequence, I wondered what kind of genius our editor would have to be to piece things together coherently.

Based on what I was seeing, I also prayed that the Writers Guild didn't have some kind of minimum quality standard in terms of membership admission. As it turns out, I had nothing to worry about. They don't.

One afternoon we were running ahead of schedule. The first assistant director suggested that we move up a limousine scene we had expected to shoot the following day. There was one problem: the car was on the set, but the actor who had been cast as chauffeur was not. After some discussion, the production manager instructed the wardrobe person to find someone who could wear the costume already tailored to fit the actor who had been hired to play the chauffeur. The wardrobe person inconspicuously walked around the set trying to determine whether anyone with dark hair could fit a 15-inch neck, 33-inch sleeve, and 31-inch waist uniform. I would have guessed these measurements were quite common. Indeed, when some of the extras saw me putting on the costume, several claimed they could wear it.

Although I was only shot from the rear as I opened the door to allow Mitch and his date to exit the limousine, for a few minutes I became the center of attention. The production manager actually approached me to say thanks.

Finished with my work in the scene, I began speaking to one extra who had been smiling at me throughout the shot. She looked extremely familiar, though for the life of me I could not place her. Her name was Candy. She told me that she had recently arrived from Massachusetts, after graduating from college as a drama major.

"Isn't your name Susan?" I asked when it finally hit me.

"Yes," she said. "Candy is my stage name. How did you know?"

"We took Don Blake's screenwriting class together. My name is Sheldon Green."

"Sheldon!" she said. "My God, I thought you were a director. You're an actor, too?"

"No," I said. "I'm a writer. I wrote this."

"You? You wrote this?"

I nodded.

"Stop pulling my leg!"

I picked up a copy of the screenplay to show her my name on the title page.

"It's brilliant," she said. "Who would have imagined?"

I hadn't liked Susan in class. I remembered the way her clique had laughed at me following Don Blake's scathing critique of my surf association/life insurance pitch. I had a different feeling speaking to her on the set.

"I have to get out of my costume," I said.

"Here," she said, handing me her phone number. "Give me yours, too. Let's talk soon. Keep in touch, okay?"

Susan/Candy called me that very same evening. After confirming I had no other plans, she invited me over.

"What are you going to do with me?" she asked when I walked in the door.

"Nothing," I said.

"You can do whatever you want."

I guess I hadn't understood the question.

⤴

The next morning I went straight to the location of the day's shoot. To my surprise, the only member of the company present was a young woman who introduced herself as our new craft service person. Since she had no idea what was going on either, we walked to a pay phone together and I called the office.

"Production," a male voice I didn't recognize said.

"Is Phil there?" I asked.

"Who is it?"

"Is Phil there?"

"Who is it?"

I winked at the craft service girl. "It's Sheldon Green."

"What company do you work for?"

"I wrote the screenplay."

"You what?"

"I wrote the screenplay, goddamn it!"

"Sheldon?"

"Yes."

"I don't think we've met. My name is Frank. Frank LeVine. I'll be working in the office, helping any way I can—at least until school starts. I love what you did with your script. Do you mind if I ask you a few questions? I've been thinking about writing a screenplay myself. How did you get your idea? Did it take long to write? Some people say that you have to use note cards. Some people say you should make an outline. How did you do it?"

"Frank," I said, "let's discuss this another time. I'm out here on location. Where is everybody?"

"Oh," he said. "I tried to reach you this morning. You weren't home."

"What's going on?"

"Mitch One is sick. He's feeling better now. Phil decided to schedule a one o'clock call."

"Mitch One is sick," I relayed to the craft service person, "but he's feeling better. We have a one o'clock call."

I liked the way she was looking at me.

"Do you have plans between now and then?" I asked her.

She shook her head to indicate that she didn't.

"My treat."

"You really know how to handle yourself," she said as we walked to my car. "Don't you?"

"There's no reason you would know this," I said. "But I've been around the block a few times."

Returning to the set after lunch, Susan/Candy was waiting for me by the catering truck. "Excuse me," I said to the craft service girl and ambled over.

"These are for you," Susan/Candy said, handing me a tin full of cookies and hugging me. Some crew members wolf-whistled and applauded. Susan/Candy acted as if she wanted me to kiss her.

"Thanks for the cookies," I said, embarrassed as hell. "I'll see you later."

"I thought I'd hang around," she said. "I worked on this picture for a few days myself, you know. Just let me know if you need anything."

"Do what you want," I said. About forty-five minutes later, I noticed that she was gone.

Mitch One made his appearance an hour-and-a-half late. His wrangler announced it was going to be necessary to cut back on the amount of Coke Mitch was drinking until he was off it altogether. "A chimpanzee is not designed to drink Coke," he said.

"We'll get the little guy off the stuff," Phil responded. "In the meantime, can we get started?"

Mitch One's handler wasn't finished. He asked that Prescott lower his voice when addressing Mitch. In situations where Prescott might once have explained things more patiently, he was now simply raising his voice and repeating the same instructions. Comparing some publicity shots taken during the first days Prescott was on the job with what we were seeing now, I knew that the special bond between director and chimp was a thing of the past.

"Prescott's background is in commercials," Phil said to Max who stopped by for a look. "I don't know if he has the stamina."

"He'll make it," Max said.

"He'd better," Phil replied. "We've got two chimps, only one director."

The day ended with Mitch One screaming and hollering from the top of the camera crane brought in for the purpose of taking a panoramic shot. Phil stood at the bottom of the crane, screaming and hollering back.

I arrived home to a shock of my own. Opening the door to my apartment, I saw Susan/Candy standing barefoot in the kitchen. She wore a skimpy top and skintight black cycling shorts. She was stirring something on the stove.

"Doug let me in," she said. "Do you like chili? Have a seat and relax. You're home." She walked over and gave me a big, wet, sloppy kiss.

Jesus.

A Loss

As Mitch One's capacity to concentrate on work diminished, the tricks Prescott used to tease him out of his frequent lapses became more cruel. Sometimes Prescott would show Mitch One a can of Coke before beginning work on a scene, indicating he could have it if he performed satisfactorily. However, when the scene was completed, Prescott would instead hand Mitch a can filled with water. Mitch would stomp and scream when he realized it wasn't "the real thing." Prescott pushed Mitch until he couldn't take it anymore. Then we had to give him the Coke.

Mitch Two was not a money player. He had a tendency to sulk when under the lights. The success of our entire project rested on Mitch One's tiny shoulders. "He plays it with just the right amount of schmaltz," Phil said about Mitch One. "We're lucky to have him."

Of course, the product placement people thought that Mitch One was the greatest thing to happen since the easy-open aluminum can. Photographers were constantly on the set popping flashbulbs. This also upset the chimp.

Mitch One began to stash cans of Coke in and around the set. During one scene shot at the high school, Mitch One pulled out a can of Coke he had hidden under a table and started to drink. One of the extras said, "Look, Mitch loves Coke!" The camera was rolling. No one broke character. The scene worked so well that the talent agency handling Coke's worldwide advertising decided to launch an aggressive campaign using the footage. Prescott rewarded the extra with a few more lines, enabling the young man to become a member of the Screen Actors Guild. Seeing this, several other extras began to improvise, popping off with what they thought were great lines so often that the extras coordinator, Prescott, the production manager, and Phil each had to make a speech so that we could get back to the business at hand.

Max invited me to sit in on a meeting scheduled one morning to review the status of "Mitch and Me" with the studio's marketing department. As Phil, Max, and I walked to the office building on the far side of the lot, Phil claimed that the studio was already selling us down the river.

Max did not agree.

"Well," Phil said, "if they're going to spend a fortune on advertising, how will the movie ever make a profit?"

"Get with it, Phil!" Max said. "The days when you could get by with a couple publicity stunts are over. A picture needs media dollars to compete. You know that."

Ross Krieger, executive vice president of domestic marketing, did not keep us waiting long. He dressed so well, I felt like a slob standing next to him.

"I don't have to tell you," he said, escorting us down the hallway to his office. "The product placement people are extremely happy with what you've done."

"They should be," Max said. "We're shooting a ninety-minute commercial."

Before getting down to the specifics concerning our movie, Ross took a moment to fill us in on what he did. "Motion picture marketing," he explained, "is no longer a seat-of-the-pants operation. Sophisticated techniques and strategies are used today to position each and every motion picture to its best possible advantage."

Ross continued by suggesting that certain filmmakers already have an audience for their movies. He cited Steven Spielberg as the best example and said that, in a more limited way, Woody Allen had once been another. "Any other filmmaker who used Woody Allen's material would have never received the acclaim he garnered." Ross paused. "Until he crossed the line, if you know what I mean."

"What are you trying to tell us?" Phil asked.

"We don't have that kind of head start with your film," Ross said, "meaning someone's name that would give us a leg up. We need to find those elements within your film itself that we can build upon—identifiable elements that will attract an audience. We'll use the results from the screenings we've scheduled to determine exactly who your target audience is."

"That's easy," Max said. "Our film appeals to people who read *The New York Times Book Review*."

There was silence. Then Phil burst out laughing. Max started laughing. I started laughing. Finally, Ross laughed, too.

"Enough with the demographics humor," Phil said. "What was it you said about screenings that have already been scheduled?"

"You didn't get a copy?" Ross seemed surprised. "I'm sure we 'cc'd' you on that. We talked about it, no?" He pulled out a memo. "This Thursday in Seattle. Orange County next Friday."

"This Thursday?" Phil asked. "What are you going to show?"

"Well, we weren't expecting to screen the final print. Don't tell me there's been another delay? We're pressing the release date as it is, don't you think?"

Phil and Max looked at each other. "Do you like the title of our picture?" Max asked. "Or do you think we should change it?"

"I love it," Ross said. "It's real. It's accessible. Besides it's too late to change it."

"What is the title of our picture?" Max asked.

Ross looked at his appointment book. "You're kidding me! Phil Fried? 'Mitch and . . .' My God, am I embarrassed. I got you totally confused with my two o'clock appointment: Phil Freeman. I've just been overwhelmed. Can you imagine?" His face turned bright red. Ross activated his intercom. "Cynthia," he ordered, "I need to see the file for 'Mitch and Me' at once."

"Cynthia's out today," a voice responded.

"Isn't that something?" Ross said. "Cynthia has to be out today. You know, it's funny. I'll bet I speak to Phil Freeman on the phone every day, but we've never met."

"Where are we?" Phil Fried asked.

"Where are we?" Ross repeated. "I'll tell you where we are." He rustled through the papers on his desk, scanning one of them briefly. "The positive is that you have a clear concept with potentially broad appeal. The negative, and I'd like this comment to remain within these four walls, is that your movie lacks a white male lead. The lead you do have generates zero name recognition. Had any of you heard of Mitch—what is this? Had any of you heard of Mitch—I can't read this writing. Had any of you heard of Mitch Uno before you got involved with the picture?"

"Mitch Uno?" Phil asked.

Phil, Max, and I looked at each other and laughed. None of us knew Mitch One's real name as it was.

"What do you think of our title?" Phil asked again when we were able to resume. "Now that we're all on the same page."

"I like it," Ross replied in a tone of voice that sounded as if he was trying to reestablish authority. "We'll test it if you want. But hands-off sounds good to me. Let's leave it alone."

"If Ross Krieger likes the title," Phil said when the elevator doors closed and the three of us were by ourselves, "we definitely have to change it." He looked at me. "See what you can come up with."

I nodded.

"And fast."

"I'm going to make a few phone calls above," Max said. "I want to see if we can get someone else to work with us on the marketing."

"If you think it'll do any good," Phil replied. "Those guys at the top are geniuses at playing both sides of the fence."

Max wasn't listening. "That monkey is going to destroy us," he said. "And I don't mean Mitch!"

The elevator doors jerked open. "How about lunch?" Phil asked.

"The Iris?" Max replied.

"Sounds good to me," Phil said.

"Sheldon?"

"Sounds good to Sheldon, too," Phil answered.

Max Planck knows a few things about wine. He even ordered a second bottle so we could compare its taste with that of the first bottle we drank.

During our meal several people stopped by the table to
say hello to Max. They didn't talk about movies at all, but
thanked Max for his help with various charity events and
asked about his family. While Max was speaking with one
of these people, Phil told me that Max had been married
to the same woman for more than forty years. And Phil
told me something else. There's a floor of a UCLA hospital
named in his honor: The Max Planck Institute for the
Study of Sinus Conditions.

As we sat eating lunch that day, I think it finally sank
in that I was the author of a screenplay being made into a
major motion picture. To hear some people talk, this was
an event which never happened in real life.

I'm sure I became overconfident. Once or twice on the
set I even told someone who was trying to sell me on a
premise for the next great American screenplay, "Enough
with the brilliant ideas already!" Then winking and
laughing and throwing an arm over that person's shoulders I'd make an invitation to go out for a drink. "Let's
talk about it in my office," I would say.

I've often wondered if what happened next was a pun-
ishment of sorts for my arrogance. Just when I was beginning to feel so good about my world, disaster struck:
Mitch One passed away in his sleep, a victim of duodenal
ulcer hemorrhaging, a condition complicated by his
overindulgence in the drink he loved, Coke.

A pall hung over the set. Markie Lyle cried uncontrol-
lably. We did what we could to console him, but then
Mitch Two would come tearing around the corner and
Markie would fall apart all over again.

There was confusion about how we should proceed.
Phil and Max both feared we might be in for some

negative publicity. They were especially concerned that "Mitch and Me" might get tagged within the industry as a "problem picture."

Furthermore, none of us believed that Mitch Two was up to the task. The production manager suggested that we bring in another, more experienced chimp to fill Mitch One's shoes. He also thought we should bring in a more experienced screenwriter to fill mine. I think what hurt most was when I overheard him say that this should have been done in the beginning.

Max Planck pointed out that it was nonsense for us to lose our heads. "Mitch and Me" was almost a wrap; there were only six days left to shoot.

I felt proud to be associated with Max. He didn't get excited when it looked as if things were going our way, and he didn't get upset when it looked as if they weren't. "Inch by inch," he liked to say. "So much for today's inch. Don't worry. We'll think of something."

And we did. We decided to proceed with Mitch Two as if nothing had happened. Meanwhile, those who could be spared from the set—Phil, Max, and I—holed up in the bungalow to assess exactly where we stood in terms of what was in the can and what remained to be shot. Phil and Max became temporarily unavailable to studio executives, to the bank, to the completion bond company, and to anyone except Prescott until they could speak with greater confidence about our situation.

As luck would have it—and perhaps as could be expected with so few days of production remaining on the schedule—most of the key scenes involving Mitch had already been shot.

However, a movie is not only a matter of celluloid, sound, and light, but also of people, spirit, and cooperation. The cooperation was there—God knows our people were willing—but the loss of Mitch One was a devastating blow to our collective spirit. Quite simply, everyone involved with the picture had fallen head over heels in love with him. Logistically we would manage, dumb luck was on our side there. But how to hold ourselves together emotionally was another question. Phil understood that to get our project back on track he was going to have to do something about cast and crew morale. And do so quickly.

Phil decided that we would knock off early that day. He also declared that we would hold a memorial service for Mitch One. The production manager personally informed each member of the company that a sunrise service would begin at six o'clock the next morning. He told me three times.

Out of respect for Mitch One, everyone arrived on time. Phil, wearing sunglasses, stood in front of the group. After leading a silent prayer, he spoke a few words about what Mitch One had meant to him personally.

Phil said first he would always remember Mitch One for the joy he brought into the world. He said that Mitch One reminded him about the need to play and the importance of being true to oneself, about never having to pretend to be someone else. Phil recalled for the mourners that when he first heard the idea of a movie about an escaped chimp who is mistaken for a foreign exchange student he thought (a) that's totally ridiculous, and (b) how will we ever find a chimp who can handle the part? "Well," Phil said, "we had a chimp who could handle the part, all right." In this way, Phil added, Mitch One helped him to realize that he could be wrong, something four wives had yet to accomplish.

There was some laughter following this remark. Laughter amid the tears.

Phil suggested that in a moment like this, when we have a chance to reflect on what life means, we should look into ourselves and see what it is that we—meaning each one of us—can do to be better people. In his own case, Phil pledged, he was going to be more honest. Phil said that he had grown tired of the old Hollywood bullshit and that he was challenging himself personally to tell the truth about everything, to be straight with people, and to really "tell it like it is."

Phil invited the entire cast and crew to join him in his resolution. He asked each one of us to be honest with each other at all times, whether it concerned our grief about having lost Mitch One to substance abuse, or whether it related to our guilt about not sharing a little more off the top in our everyday lives. "We all have just a few days left on this shoot," Phil said, "but maybe during that short time we can make a fresh start, take something of value into the world that will stay with us long after we hear 'It's a wrap' for the last time. Let's be better people, people."

Phil asked all members of the group to join together holding hands so that Morris Goulding—scheduled to be with us that day in his role as high school principal, but who had recently been featured in another movie as a rabbi—could lead the final prayer. At this point, the first assistant cameraman noticed that Mitch Two wasn't present. He asked if it wouldn't be appropriate to have Mitch Two and his wrangler join us for the conclusion of our service. Phil agreed it was important to have them with us. He said that Mitch Two would help us to remember that every ending is also a new beginning.

"Where is Mitch Two?" he asked.

Kimberley offered to check. When she returned, everyone had gathered in a circle and was holding hands. "He's in his trailer," she said.

"Let's get him out," Phil replied.

Kimberley looked pained by this request.

"Well?"

Kimberley bit her bottom lip.

"What's he doing?" Phil asked.

Kimberley shook her head slightly as if she were trying to signal Phil.

"What's he doing?" Phil repeated.

"Mitch Two is in his trailer," Kimberley answered finally. "He's masturbating."

Emes, The Truth

Following the memorial service, nobody discussed the first chimp who worked on the picture. During the last few days of shooting, Mitch Two simply became Mitch. It was taboo to use the words "dead" or "death," and no one mentioned Mitch One's addiction to Coke or any possible connection between his habit and the stress to which he had been subjected during filming.

Mitch One's wrangler was actually made to feel unwelcome on the set. He stopped by ostensibly to pick up what of Mitch One's personal effects had not been in the trailer at the time of his death. I suspect the real reason he came by was that he was lonely and wanted to spend some time near the site where Mitch One had lived his last few days. Phil ignored the man as if he'd never been a member of our team at all. I spent most of one morning trying to cheer him up. And I spent most of another with Markie Lyle doing the same.

It may seem judgmental on my part, but I must say that neither the product placement people nor the people from the advertising agency appeared to care that Mitch One had died. The way these folks began to fawn over Mitch Two—immediately scheduling a special session with photographer Herb Ritts and discussing arrangements for an upcoming national tour to promote both product and film—one might have easily forgotten that Mitch One was ever around.

Of course a few people new to the project had no idea what was going on. Indeed, it wasn't until the last week of production that I met Camilla. She came with a friend to work as an extra. Camilla wasn't the most beautiful woman I'd ever met, but I liked her smile. She actually grinned more than smiled—a wide face-splitting grin that showed lots of teeth. She smiled so hard that I was afraid her eyes might cross. Camilla didn't seem to be self-conscious about her looks. I liked that.

I would have asked Camilla for her phone number, but I didn't want to embarrass her in front of the wardrobe people who I knew had developed a reputation for cattiness. Frankly, I didn't want to embarrass myself by asking Camilla in front of her friend or the other extras. Being screenwriter on the project was no guarantee she would say yes. But I did notice, as we were about to wrap, that the extras coordinator had left her clipboard lying on a table. I walked by a few times in just the right way so I could memorize the phone number next to Camilla's name. Ordinarily I would have thought that this was a lousy thing to do. But the film was almost finished, and life is short. And we'd had an especially nice conversation, I felt.

I don't know what Camilla did with her free time. She was never at home. Several times when I called, there was no answer. Later someone picked up the phone, but didn't say anything. I tried speaking Spanish, "*Yo soy* Sheldon Green.*" It had been a long time since I studied the language and I knew this wasn't correct. I thought the effort would be appreciated. It wasn't. The next time I called, I introduced myself in English to someone I hoped was taking down the necessary information. I left two or three messages this way. Camilla didn't call back. The next to last time I called, the woman on the other end of the line was short with me. The last time I called, someone hung up.

It was hard for me to concentrate on other things. Camilla was constantly on my mind. Fortunately, I was busy. Following an introduction arranged by Max Planck and wildly endorsed by Martin Falklands, an agent named Sam Strutner began to schedule appointments for me with people interested in having me write exactly the same kind of movie should "Mitch and Me" turn out to be a big hit. If it was a hit, but not a big hit, these people were interested in what I could write that featured the strong points of "Mitch and Me" but suffered none of its faults. If the movie bombed, people were willing to take a first look at anything else I might write without charging me for their time.

Driving home from the studio I decided to stop by Vons Market to pick up a copy of the tabloid that had originally displayed the headline "Chimp Tests Prove IQ of 120." I wanted to get the paper's address and send them a letter to see if that particular back issue was still available. If so, I could have it framed to hang above my sofa bed. Doug would have to take it down if he didn't want to look at it every day.

While in the supermarket, I happened to notice that bananas were on sale: *Bananas, 16¢/lb.*

"'16 Bananas,'" I said to myself out loud. "That's it!"

I rushed out of the store to the parking lot. I was halfway to my car before realizing that I hadn't paid for the paper I was carrying under my arm. I might have been arrested for shoplifting. I ran back inside to give a cashier some money and then I ran out again.

"'16 Bananas,'" I said to anyone who would listen to me. "Yes!"

The new title—"16 Bananas"—was a big hit with everybody. Fortunately, we were able to make a significant change in a scene yet to be shot. Originally I had planned for the family to celebrate Mitch's seventeenth birthday with a picnic party in the park. Expecting that this would not only be the last scene shot, but the final scene in the film as well, Phil understood how important it was to create the right spin, leaving an appropriate image with the audience, especially one connected to the movie's title. He told the production designer to spare no expense in changing Mitch's birthday from his seventeenth to his sixteenth.

The production designer told Phil not to worry. He said it would be less expensive because we would save a candle.

In factoring all the different elements into my final set of changes to the screenplay, I tried to incorporate Mitch Two's tendency to sulk and scowl when under the lights. In particular, I reworked the last scene so that when the circus handler finally catches up with Mitch, he is held off just long enough for everyone to say good-bye to Mitch, whom Jimmy accepts is going home. The scene works because what looks to be such a happy sweet sixteen party on one level is actually a bittersweet farewell party on another.

The only character in the movie still dumb enough to think that Mitch is a foreign exchange student is the high school principal. In fact, he remarks that although Mitch has improved his English comprehension, he has yet to utter one word of English.

Due to the circumstances, it was agreed that we would not have a wrap party. Totally exhausted at the completion of filming, cast and crew said good-bye to each other, promising to keep in touch.

I was so wound up that I thought about going out for a drink by myself. I chose to drive home instead.

Not five minutes after I walked in the door, Doug answered the phone. "It's for you," he said.

"If her name is Susan or Candy—" I began, but he shook his head.

"Her name is Camilla, big boy."

Camilla told me that she had been out of town. She was surprised that I had called, but sounded pleased, almost flattered.

"How did you get my number?" she asked.

"I took it off the paperwork on the set."

"That was smart."

"I'm glad you think so."

After we had spoken for a while, the whole time with Doug eavesdropping from the kitchen, I asked Camilla if she was free over the weekend.

"I'm free," she said.

"Should we make a tentative plan?"

"I don't make tentative plans."

"How does Saturday look?"

"What time?"

Before hanging up Camilla said, "Thanks again for calling."

I said, "Thank you."

Doug removed the spoon from his mouth and plunged it into the pint of Ben & Jerry's he was holding. "What happened to Susan?" he asked. "Or should I say Candy?"

"Did something happen?"
"You should know."
"Why do you care?"
"Just asking."
"Doug?"
"Yes?"
"What are you doing this weekend?"
"I'm going to my folks," he said.
"Too bad I can't make it."

Camilla wore an adorable black-and-pink polka dot on white mini-skirt and a pair of simple leather sandals with no socks or stockings. When she got into my car, she immediately reached across the seat to unlock my door.

"Don't worry," I said. "It's broken."

I suggested we choose a movie playing nearby—a movie that wasn't epic in terms of running time. The point, I felt, was to spend the evening with each other.

For dinner, Camilla ordered a small salad with Italian dressing and half a chicken salad sandwich on whole wheat bread, lightly toasted. I ordered a dinner salad with blue cheese dressing and a whole chicken salad sandwich on whole wheat bread, also lightly toasted. When the check came, Camilla offered to split it with me. I insisted on paying, so she left the tip. I was surprised how comfortably we seemed to get along. Even on our first date, we appeared to have moved well past the awkward stage when two people are checking each other out, deciding whether they want to see each other again. I suppose we'd already decided.

Later that evening, when we sat down together on my sofa bed, I was just amazed that such a lovely person could be there beside me. Camilla excused herself for a minute to go into the bathroom. When she returned, I felt that she gave me a kind of all-clear signal without being too obvious about it.

I kissed her. For some reason, we both laughed. I kissed her again.

Camilla was my date when we previewed *16 Bananas* at a shopping center in Costa Mesa, a city south of Los Angeles. I thought that Camilla was extremely animated and gracious with everyone she met without seeming at all desperate to make a good impression. I don't think I've ever been happier than I was the night of the screening.

Camilla and I stood in the lobby with the VIP's until an usher led us down the aisle and removed the masking tape border from the specially reserved row where we were supposed to sit.

A man from the research company stepped to the front of the theater. "Thank you for coming to this evening's preview of *16 Bananas*," he said. "What you will see is a work-in-progress. If there are scratches on the screen or problems with the soundtrack, please assume that when the movie is released into theaters these things will be cleared up."

"Let's see the fucking chimp," someone from the audience shouted.

"I have one more request," the man continued. "Please remain in your seats immediately after the film has been completed."

I think he may have been planning to say something else, but the lights went down and the movie began.

EXTERIOR. AERIAL SHOT. A TRAVELING CIRCUS PUTS UP A TENT IN AN UNDISTINGUISHED AMERICAN TOWN.

CREDITS: "A Prescott Lansing Film / Executive Producer Max Planck / Co-Producer Ethan Albright III / Produced by Cullen McCarthy & Philip S. Fried."

There was some "spontaneous" cheering and applause when Phil's name flashed across the screen. This was because of all the family members and friends he had invited in an effort to influence the screening results, despite the stipulation that we were not supposed to know anyone there.

CREDITS: "Story by Sheldon Greene / Screenplay by Prescott Lansing & Sheldon Greene / Directed by Prescott Lansing."

Screenplay by *Prescott Lansing* and Sheldon Greene? I gasped for air. How many hours would Martin Falklands bill me to straighten out that? I wasn't making enough money on this movie to pay my attorney what it was costing me to get through it.

"They misspelled your name," Camilla whispered.

"Don't worry about it," I said. "They'll fix that for free."

Camilla gave me a little nudge and took my hand.

Once I calmed down, watching *16 Bananas* with an audience for the first time was a truly wonderful experience. My two favorite moments: Camilla standing behind the cash register in the high school cafeteria, and the shot in which I open the limousine door for Mitch and his prom date.

More seriously—from a screenwriter's point of view— I was pleased by how well the scenes worked related to Mom's part-time job at McDonald's. Without giving away so much that it spoils the film for those who have yet to see it, Mom decides that if she can find a part-time job it will be a big help with the family's finances. But she's afraid that Dad's feelings will be hurt and so she confides in her daughter Jenny. Jenny has been doing fine with her own part-time job at McDonald's and doesn't miss the school band at all. Jenny encourages her mother to apply for the job.

Mom's interview with the manager is tough. "We've had mother-daughter teams that were marvelous," he says. "And we've had some that didn't work out at all."

"I hardly see Jenny these days as it is," Mom says. "Sometimes I wonder if we're even related."

The manager responds by saying that his personal bias is against hiring members of the same family, but because Jenny is such a good egg, and up for promotion, he will make an exception.

Jenny is soon promoted to assistant manager, at least partially on the basis of having recruited another fine employee—her mother. Therefore Jenny, who is still in high school, gets to supervise her mother at work and tell her what to do. Mom can't refuse Jenny's orders or talk back. Not only is she proud of her daughter, but it's not so easy to find a good job these days. This was the set-up for lots of great moments where Jenny, who has suffered such indignities at home as having to take out the garbage, do her homework after dinner, and stay in on weeknights, has a chance to tell her mother that she is not working fast enough. And in a scene the audience just loved, Jenny gets to grade her mother on a standard evaluation form for things like personal hygiene, attitude, presentation, work habits, and team spirit.

Realities being what they are, Jenny is caught between a rock and a hard place. She wants to be nice to her mother who has developed a reputation for over-salting the french fries and failing to clean up properly after using the milk shake dispenser. But Jenny also has to be fair to the company. And honest.

Mom bristles. The audience screams.

To hear our audience hooting and hollering, a person might wonder whether the chimps were up on the screen or sitting in the theater.

My reaction did prove at least one thing: contrary to what a college psychology professor of mine once said, a person can have more than one perception, experience, feeling, thought, or sensation at the same time. I say this because watching the audience respond, I felt simultaneously exhilarated and discouraged, totally validated and absolutely worthless. The movie was truly great—and nothing but a load of crap.

When the picture was over, ushers rushed down the aisles distributing questionnaires before the audience could exit. But people showed no urgency to leave. There was more applause. Even allowing for all the invitations to the screening Kimberley had made on Phil's behalf, the clapping seemed sincere in the sense that it appeared to spread throughout the room.

Everyone connected with the production waited patiently in the theater lobby while the market research people tabulated the questionnaires. At least three minutes passed before a series of mini pow-wows broke out regarding the credits.

For the record, this issue was settled by the end of the week, following consultations with agents, lawyers, studio attorneys, and the Writers Guild. In the final credits, Phil's name appears before Cullen's, and the screenwriting credit reads: *Written by Sheldon Green.*

While we were standing in the lobby waiting for the hard numbers, a studio executive I'd only met for the first time that evening started raving about what a great job we had done. And when the numbers actually came in, he kept saying, "I told you. I told you, didn't I? We are in very good shape with this picture. Now we just have to sell the hell out of it. Where's Ross Krieger?" He just wouldn't stop talking about what a terrific movie we had made.

As Phil would later explain to me, one thing that separates many successful studio executives from the wanna-be's is the sincere belief that what they are doing constitutes good work.

Max had only one comment before leaving. "When you spend this much money making a movie," he said, "the sound should come out at the same time the characters move their mouths."

An usher handed me two *Look, Mitch loves Coke!* T-shirts as Camilla and I walked out the door.

The next morning we were supposed to hold a meeting in the bungalow to discuss the results from the screening and consider what changes, if any, should be made to the movie before its release. However, with the brouhaha about the credits raging, Phil quickly instructed Kimberley to reschedule the meeting for two o'clock sharp. We finally got down to business about three forty-five, but there was nothing to discuss. We all knew that there wasn't going to be any serious reshooting. The most worrisome development was the one studio executive who had surfaced at the screening and who was trying to ingratiate himself with Phil and Max. He thought that *16 Bananas* wasn't clear enough to be an effective title.

His proposal, "16 Bananas and a Little Chimp," did receive a brief review before being rejected by a committee of three: Phil, his wife, and their three year-old daughter. With the sweet smell of success in the air, Mrs. Fried determined that now was the time to clarify her contribution to the picture and to let everyone know she was available regarding major artistic decisions—her first pronouncement being: "Don't change the title."

Although I was pleased to get away from the bungalow that afternoon, I soon realized there would be no escape. *16 Bananas* was no longer only my movie. It belonged to everyone now. *People* displayed a picture of Mitch One (taken by a *paparazzo* on the set) on its cover under a headline reading, "Hollywood's Newest Star?" *US* countered with a story about "America's 10 Greatest Chimps." *Life* included a photo-essay featuring celebrity pets and their owners.

The studio decided to move up our release date. Martin Falklands confided to me that he had bet on the success of our movie with a play on the studio's stock in the options market. He decided to do this after coming home from work one day and hearing his nine-year-old son discussing the movie while playing Sega CD with his friends.

Unfortunately, it wasn't long before one of the tabloids caught wind of the fact that Mitch One had passed away during production. *People*, seeking to downplay its nomination of a dead chimp as "Newcomer of the Year," shifted its focus to a number of related issues, including the proper caretaking of animals. *National Enquirer* countered with a story claiming that Mitch One was not only alive, but was female, pregnant, and doing a year of volunteer work in hopes of bolstering her chances of getting into medical school.

I guess it was inevitable that hard questions related to Mitch One's demise would arise sooner or later. Instead of the many hoped-for phone calls from parties interested in future projects that I was not, but might have been working on, I received an inordinate number of calls angling for inside information about what happened to Mitch One and the parallel story regarding his rumored Coke habit.

I will say that Phil and Kimberley were absolutely at their best during this time. There were a number of complicated legal questions to sort out, such as the exclusive arrangement between Mitch One and the production company regarding sequel work. Martin Falklands explained our position: clearly a contract between a production company and a dead chimp is unenforceable. Privately, he was less confident. Because Mitch One had not signed the contract himself, the agreement was technically between the production company and Mitch One's wrangler. If this indeed proved to be the case, Mitch One's trainer had the studio over a barrel in terms of sequel production. Phil was concerned about millions of dollars of potential future revenues lost because it turned out some guy he once snubbed had an exclusive contract—and worse, no A-chimp to go with it.

After a while there was an outpouring of sympathy for Mitch Two. Frankly, I felt it was about time. Here was an understudy who had suffered for weeks in the shadow of a major talent. Mitch Two was not a chimp blessed with much natural ability, but he was a journeyman. I will always remember him as one who did the little things right. He cared.

I don't want to minimize the stress we were under. If the public relations people hadn't been such a great group of kids, I don't know how we would have made it.

But we did.

We were the number one grossing box office hit for eighteen consecutive weeks.

Variety and *The Hollywood Reporter* treated us to some gorgeous ink: "Monkey Business!" "Bananza!" "Simian Sez: 'More Screens!'"

Our soundtrack went multi-platinum.

Lunch boxes, sweatshirts, decals, "spin-offs," and "tie-ins" appeared on retail shelves everywhere. Action figures spilled from cereal boxes and peaked out of fast-food bags.

Critics saw things in our picture I hadn't known existed. "A miracle," wrote the *Los Angeles Times*, "sensitively written. Charming."

"Full of wit and wisdom," claimed *USA Today*. "The feel-good movie of the year."

The New Yorker called *16 Bananas* "an important motion picture," and used the word "sanguine" in its review four times. (I'm still not sure what that word means.)

Despite concerns about how an American family's inability to distinguish between a foreign exchange student and a chimpanzee would play overseas, our movie made more money in its international release than it did in the United States. We even won a Golden Something Award at a European film festival.

There was talk throughout the industry about a new "monkey genre." Studios and independent production companies put chimp pictures into development all over town. Screenwriters discussed the "monkey formula." Word was that with half a concept and the right chimp, success was guaranteed.

Phil and Max were more sober in their assessment of the situation. Together we discussed, debated, and rejected many possible concepts for an imagined sequel we affectionately referred to as "17 Bananas." It went without saying, we could have any primate in town. But somehow the energy wasn't there.

"The problem in life," Max counseled, "is never the good ideas—there are so few—and it's never the bad ideas because everybody knows what to do about those.

The problem in life is the mediocre ideas. Those are the ones that kill you."

"Amen," Phil said.

"I haven't given you much advice," Max said to me, "but I'm going to make a suggestion regarding the sequel. Why don't we let *them* screw it up? Because, believe me, they're going to anyway."

He looked at his watch. "The Iris?"

Seated at his table at the back of the Iris, Max announced that *16 Bananas* would be his last picture. "This is it," he said. "It's a young people's business these days. I don't have it anymore."

"I've heard that from you before," Phil said. "I'll believe it when I see it."

Certainly Max looked terrific. If anyone appeared to need the rest, it was Phil.

I asked if we should have included our Japanese investors in the credits.

"They don't want the publicity," Max said.

"I don't understand."

"This is the first Japanese company that's ever made money in Hollywood. If word gets out, they're going to have to explain to everyone else in their country how they did it."

"I have another question," I said, turning to Phil to apologize. "Please don't take this the wrong way."

"Go ahead."

"Looking back," I said to Max, "there were a lot of other, more obvious places you could have gone when this project began. Why Phil?"

Max didn't pause. "It was his turn."

Phil acknowledged Max's comment by raising his glass. There was a twinkle in his eye I hadn't seen often enough. Phil turned my way. "Is there anything you'd like to ask me?"

"Yes," I said. "There is one thing. What does the 'S' in Philip S. Fried stand for?"

"Solvent," Max said. He roared with laughter.

"Maybe I should use two S's," Phil replied.

"By the way," I asked, "is it realistic to think I might make any money off the 'net points' defined in my contract?"

"I've seen a lot of definitions," Phil said. "I haven't seen too many profits."

"Think of it this way," Max added. "You'll find what you've made from net points in heaven one day, along with the socks you lost at the laundromat and the puppy your parents wouldn't let you keep."

"Well," I said, "If I did it once, maybe I can do it again."

"Don't push your luck," Max said. "You'll only make yourself unhappy. If it's meant to be, it will happen."

"I have an idea," I said, "although at the moment it's not much more than a set-up. Phil, you're good with this kind of thing. Tell me what you think."

I began slowly, working both hands earnestly in support of my well-rehearsed pitch: "A secret team of highly-trained commandos handcuffed for years by Congressional oversight committees is brought out of the shadows by a president desperate to checkmate an equally skilled group of neo-Nazis bent on attacking our nation's capital."

Phil took a deep breath. "Max?"

"I'm retired," Max said.

"It's commercial," Phil said finally. "I don't know if I like it."

"You'll like the title," I replied.

"Yes?"

I could hardly keep a straight face. "'Social Impact!'"

"I'm going to social impact *you*," Phil said.

"Don't worry," I said. "You already have."

The three of us talked for a long time that afternoon. When the waiter brought our check, there was a bit of a tussle. In the end, Max and Phil let me win.

When I arrived home, Doug was having sex with Susan/Candy on the living room floor. "You have no right to say anything," he claimed. "I don't owe you a thing."

"I came by to see you, Sheldon," Susan/Candy said. "I'm so sorry."

I did my best to act hurt and confused. "Take your things and get out of here. Both of you. Doug, you can pick up the rest of your stuff tomorrow."

"Sheldon," she said, "please. Listen to me." Stark naked, she broke her embrace with Doug and ran to where I was standing by the door.

"There's nothing to say." I looked at Doug. "Tomorrow," I reiterated as I was leaving. "Out of here!"

As fate would have it, Doug and Susan/Candy decided to move in together. Based on Doug's triumphant expression as he piled his things into a couple of grocery bags, I believe he felt that he was exacting some measure of revenge from me. I had no intention of letting him think otherwise.

Martin Falklands called the week the movie opened to ask if I wanted to continue paying him on an inconvenient hourly basis or whether I would prefer to pay him a straight five percent of my income as had become customary among clients of the more successful attorneys in town. "Less hassle," he said.

"For whom?" I asked.

"For both of us. It's a more sophisticated way of doing business. It means we're on the same side."

I asked him whom I should pay for advice about that. He laughed.

In retrospect, I know that having Martin Falklands in my corner was a major reason that things worked out so well for me. I considered sending him a bottle of Champagne. Oh, fuck it, I thought, he got paid plenty.

Howard called to check in with me the week the movie opened as well. He told me that he had burned out at traffic school and was back at Graphic Toner, which had relocated to another part of town. Howard also confessed that he was thinking about becoming a screenwriter. "Is there a secret?" he asked.

I had to think about it. In fact, I couldn't shake the question. Was there a secret? That evening I took out my screenplay. I did notice one thing: no speech had more than three lines. Most had only one. No line of dialogue had more than ten words. Most had less than five.

Personally, I feel very lucky. Thanks to the success of *16 Bananas*, I'll most likely work again. One day I might even have something to say.

As for Camilla and myself, we seem to get along just fine. I'm sure I don't know why.